PUFFIN BOOKS

Calamity with the Fiend

Sheila Lavelle was born in Gateshead, County Durham, in 1939. When she was a child she spent all her time reading anything she could get her hands on and from the age of ten began to write plays, stories and poetry.

She married in 1958 and had two sons. When her children started school she returned to the writing that had been put on hold and sold some stories to a magazine. At the same time she trained as a teacher and taught in infant schools in Birmingham for ten years. After an illness Sheila Lavelle gave up teaching to write full time. Her first book, *Ursula Bear*, was published in 1977.

Sheila Lavelle now lives in a cottage near the sea in Galloway, Scotland, with her husband and two border collies. She is now also a grandmother! Her days are spent writing in the morning and walking her dogs in the afternoon.

D0488736

Other books by Sheila Lavelle

MY BEST FIEND
THE FIEND NEXT DOOR
TROUBLE WITH THE FIEND

In Young Puffin

FETCH THE SLIPPER
HARRY'S AUNT
THE STRAWBERRY-JAM PONY
URSULA BEAR

Calamity with the Fiend

Sheila Lavelle

Illustrated by
Margaret Chamberlain

PUFFIN BOOKS

PUFFIN BOOKS

Published by the Penguin Group
Penguin Books Ltd, 27 Wrights Lane, London W8 5TZ, England
Penguin Books USA Inc., 375 Hudson Street, New York, New York 10014, USA
Penguin Books Australia Ltd, Ringwood, Victoria, Australia
Penguin Books Canada Ltd, 10 Alcorn Avenue, Toronto, Ontario, Canada M4V 3B2
Penguin Books (NZ) Ltd, 182–190 Wairau Road, Auckland 10, New Zealand

Penguin Books Ltd, Registered Offices: Harmondsworth, Middlesex, England

First published by Hamish Hamilton Ltd 1993
Published in Puffin Books 1994
5 7 9 10 8 6

Text copyright © Sheila Lavelle, 1993
Illustrations copyright © Margaret Chamberlain, 1993
All rights reserved

The moral right of the author has been asserted

Printed in England by Clays Ltd, St Ives plc
Filmset in Baskerville

Chapter One

Schooldays are supposed to be the happiest days of your life, but if you're stuck with a friend like Angela Mitchell they're not. If you were an angel in Heaven she'd tempt you into mischief, and persuade you to play rude songs on your harp.

We trooped into the classroom one afternoon in February when the crocuses were out in the school garden and there was a smell of spring in the air. Miss Sopwith must have been in a good mood, because she'd decided to let us do

1

art instead of the boring old nature lesson she'd promised us about the germination of seeds.

You know the one I mean. You have it every springtime, in every class in the school and teachers love it. You have to take a jam jar and line it with wet blotting paper and put dried peas in it so that you can watch them grow. It's supposed to be dead thrilling, seeing the little root come out, and then the little shoot, but it's pathetic if you ask me. Watching peas grow is about as exciting as watching the clothes go round in the washing machine. It's even worse than watching *Westenders* on the telly, according to my dad.

Anyway, when we sat down in our places we found that Miss Sopwith had been busy in the lunch hour putting bits of card and scissors and sticky paper out on our desks.

'I've just realized what day it is tomorrow, children,' she said, with an even soppier expression on her face than usual. 'It's a very special day. Can anybody tell me what it is?'

'Friday, Miss,' called out that great fat fool Laurence Parker, and everybody groaned.

'I mean apart from Friday, Laurence,' said Miss Sopwith. 'What else is it?'

I put my hand up but Angela beat me to it.

'It's February the 14th, Miss Sopwith,' she called out, with that beaming smile that grown-ups love so much because it makes all her dimples show. 'It's Valentine's Day.'

Miss Sopwith nodded. 'That's right, Angela,' she said. 'Saint Valentine's Day. It's a very ancient festival, which began hundreds of years ago in the fifteenth century.'

She told us about Saint Valentine, and about how he was a martyr who was executed for his beliefs, which seems to have been the fate of most martyrs in those days, and which is probably why there aren't any left.

'He died on February the 14th,' Miss Sopwith went on. 'And so it became the custom on that day to choose a sweetheart, or a special friend, and to send them a present in memory of Saint Valentine.'

She smiled round at the class.

'Of course we send cards rather than presents these days,' she said. 'And I know you're much too young for sweethearts . . .'

She held up her hand for silence as the boys started to stamp their feet and snigger and boo, while some of the girls giggled and nudged one another.

'But I'm sure you all have a special friend you'd like to send a card to,' Miss Sopwith continued when the noise died down. 'So I thought it would be nice if we made some this afternoon. And to make it more of a challenge, I want you to write a message inside your card which matches the design on the front.'

You could tell that the boys thought it was Old Soppy's soppiest idea yet, but as they had no choice in the matter they settled down after a minute and we all got on with it. And I found I quite enjoyed the work once I'd started.

I used a design that I'd seen in the paper shop only a few days before. First of all I cut out a big red heart from sticky paper and stuck that in the middle of the card. Then I cut a long strip from a lace paper doily and stuck that down all round the edge of the heart like a lacy frill. It took me ages to draw tiny roses in all the spaces I had left, and to colour them in with red and pink and yellow felt pens, but it was worth it, because the card looked really lovely.

When it was finished I sharpened my pencil and in my very best writing I wrote a message inside that I thought was rather neat because of the heart on the front.

HAPPY VALENTINE'S DAY

FROM THE BOTTOM OF MY HEART

'That's beautiful, Charlotte,' said Miss Sopwith. 'I'm sure your special friend will be delighted to receive that.'

Everybody leaned over and craned their necks to look, and there was a chorus of oohs and ahs. I glanced round at Angela who sits in the row behind me. She grinned at me and winked, confident that I had only one special friend and that it was her.

I grinned back, but I didn't really mean it. I still hadn't forgiven her for putting that horrible black slug in my desk the day before. If she thought I was going to send a Valentine to her she had another think coming. I'd send it to that nice David Watkins instead. It would serve her right.

I made an envelope from the sheet of white paper Miss Sopwith had provided, and sealed the card up in it. I would ask my mum for a stamp when I got home, I decided, writing David's name and address on the front. Then I slipped it into my desk so that nobody would see.

The lesson was almost over and it was getting noisy again, with everybody showing their cards to one another and laughing and jeering. Cleverclogs Laurence Parker had drawn a picture of an enormous whale, with '*We could have a WHALE of a time together!*' written inside. David Watkins had drawn a sweet little furry bear, and the message inside was '*I couldn't BEAR to be without you!*' All the girls were cooing over it, and you could tell they each hoped he'd send it to them.

Angela's card was a mess. She's not very good at drawing or cutting out, and she had only managed to make a sort of house with a door in the middle and a window at each side of the door, like they do in the babies' class. Inside she'd written '*Come to my HOUSE for tea one day!*', which Miss Sopwith didn't think was very clever at all.

'Oh dear, Angela. Couldn't you make a better effort than that?' she tutted, and Angela scowled and shoved the card in the rubbish bin, because she hates anyone to be better than her.

The bell rang for afternoon playtime and we all clattered to our feet, but Old Soppy made us sit down again because she had something important to say.

'I just want to remind you that Miss Collingwood will be showing visitors round the school tomorrow, and she wants you all to look clean and smart.' She peered at us severely over her spectacles. 'No scruffy jeans or trainers, please, boys,' she said. 'And no fancy socks or legwarmers, girls, if you don't mind.'

One or two of the girls went pink and hid their feet under their desks because there had been a craze recently for wearing all sorts of stripy, coloured and patterned socks and legwarmers to school. My mum wouldn't let me wear anything but grey, but Angela had been turning up in all sorts of things, including socks with Mickey Mouse on, and bright pink fluffy leg-warmers that made her look like a flamingo.

Miss Sopwith got up from her desk. 'I know school uniform isn't strictly compulsory in the junior classes,' she said. 'But it would look nice if you could all wear it on this occasion. And that means you, too, Angela, if you don't mind.'

She dismissed the class and we all charged out into the playground like a herd of animals escaping from the zoo. Angela followed more slowly, a brooding expression on her face.

'She's a stupid old bat,' she glowered, joining me by the gate. 'There was no need to pick on me. Plenty of other people wear fancy socks.'

She glared at the classroom window, where Miss Sopwith could be seen putting out a row of jam jars on the sill. It looked as if we were going to get that nature lesson after all.

'And she needn't have been so rude about my Valentine card, either,' said Angela. 'Stupid old bat.'

'Well, it wasn't very good, was it?' I said reasonably. 'A five-year-old could do better.'

I could have bitten my tongue out as soon as I said it, for Angela directed that icy blue gaze on me and gave me a look that turned my insides to frozen chicken livers. Then she went stomping off.

I watched nervously as she gathered all the other girls in our class into a huddle in a corner of the playground. I knew she was plotting some kind of revenge, because that awful Delilah Jones kept looking at me over her shoulder and giggling, while Angela whispered into her ear.

I worried all the rest of the afternoon, and I didn't listen to one word of the nature lesson, even though Miss Sopwith had been really inventive this time and had provided beans instead of peas for a change. Only half of my mind was in the classroom, while the other half was trying to guess what Angela was cooking up. It was bound to be something nasty, I felt sure.

The bell rang for home-time at last. After a final reminder from Miss Sopwith about school uniform, we were let out. I collected my Valentine card from my desk and set off home by myself, but to my astonishment Angela ran after me and pushed her arm through mine, as nice as ninepence.

'You can give me that Valentine now, if you like,' she said. 'It'll save you posting it.'

I shook my arm free. 'It's not for you,' I told her. 'I know you've been plotting to get me into trouble. So you can just get lost, Angela Mitchell. I'm going to send it to David Watkins, if my mum'll give me a stamp.'

Angela looked hurt. 'We weren't plotting anything against you, Charlie, honest,' she said. 'We were planning our revenge on Soppy Sopwith for being such a stupid old bat.'

I scowled at her suspiciously. 'So why did you keep me out of it?' I demanded. 'Why did you tell all the others, and not me?'

She looked even more hurt. 'You're always saying you don't want to be involved in any mischief. I thought you wouldn't want anything to do with it. And anyway, I'm telling you now, aren't I?'

So I walked home with her while she told

me the plan, and it was the craziest thing I'd ever heard. In spite of what Miss Sopwith had said about school uniform, all the girls had agreed to wear coloured socks and leg-warmers to school the next day.

'That'll show her she can't boss us around,' crowed Angela gleefully, as we turned the corner into our road. 'And it won't half show her up in front of Miss Collingwood and her visitors.'

'You can't do that,' I said. 'Not after Miss Sopwith asked us specially. She'll be furious.'

'Of course she will,' said Angela. 'That's the whole point. And there won't be a thing she can do about it, will there? She said herself that uniform isn't compuncshunry in the junior school.'

I couldn't help giggling at that.

'There's no such word as compuncshunry,' I told her. 'You mean compulsory.'

'That's what I said,' she assured me, quite unabashed. 'Compulshunry. So be sure to wear your lovely purple and green stripy socks tomorrow, won't you?'

We stopped at the front gate of Angela's

house, which is next door to mine, and she snatched the Valentine card from my hand.

'I'll post that for you, Charlie,' she said. 'I've got a first class stamp. And I'm going to Barlow with my mum, so I can make sure it doesn't miss the last post.' And off she went into the house.

I wasn't very happy about it, but it was too late to stop her. She'll probably forget to post it, I told myself gloomily, as I let myself in the back door. Just to get her own back. And all that work will have been for nothing.

But I wasn't fooled by her so-called revenge on Miss Sopwith. When I thought it over it stuck out a mile that it was only another of her tricks to get me into trouble. I was supposed to turn up in stripy socks, and I was meant to be the only one. Well, this time I wasn't going to fall for it. I'd wear my grey school socks the next day, and be a step ahead of her for once.

The next morning I dressed in my uniform as usual and went downstairs. My dad was making breakfast and my mum was reading the paper at the kitchen table. I helped myself to some Sugar Crunchies, then I jumped up from the table again as the letterbox rattled in the hall.

There were three Valentine cards. One for each of us. One for my dad from my mum. One for my mum from my dad. And one for me without a signature. A card with a sweet cuddly bear on it, and the words, '*I couldn't BEAR to be without you!*' written inside.

My mum and dad started the usual soppy kissing and cooing stuff, so I quickly swallowed the rest of my breakfast and set off for school. I was so happy I almost floated round the corner into Angela's drive. I couldn't wait to see her face when I told her that out of all the girls in the class David Watkins had sent his Valentine card to me.

I forgot all about Valentines the minute I saw her. She was coming out of the house to meet me, her satchel over her shoulder, wearing her grey school coat and black shoes, and her FLUFFY FLAMINGO-COLOURED LEG-WARMERS.

'Oh, Charlie!' she laughed, looking at my feet. 'You are a wimp. You'll be the only one in grey socks, and everybody will laugh at you.'

She was right. As we walked to school we met more and more girls from our class going in the same direction. The new girl, Jane McLachlan, who moved here last year from Scotland and talks in a lovely Scottish voice. The twins, Jenny and Josie Brown, who look so much alike that even their mother gets them mixed up. That awful spiteful Delilah Jones, who pinches you and laughs when you squeal. And my heart sank deeper and deeper into my stomach because not one of them was wearing grey school socks. They were all wearing coloured tights, stockings or leg-warmers, of all colours of the rainbow.

Everybody scoffed and jeered when they saw me. They called me a namby-pamby and a goody-goody and a teacher's pet. My face burned and I felt like crawling under a stone.

We had almost reached the school gates when Angela took pity on me.

'Here, Charlie,' she said, rummaging in her satchel. 'I guessed you might chicken out, so I've brought you some of mine.' And she held out a big red bundle that turned out to be a pair of enormous woolly socks of the brightest shade of scarlet you ever saw.

I knew Miss Sopwith wouldn't be pleased, but anything was better than being an outcast in the classroom, so I sat down on a low wall and let Angela help me change. The socks were so thick I could hardly get my shoes back on, and they were so long and heavy that when I stood up they drooped in folds around my ankles, but the other girls cheered when they saw me putting them on and I felt like one of the gang again.

The school bell rang and Angela grabbed my grey socks and stuffed them into her satchel.

'Come on, Charlie,' she urged. 'We don't want to be late.'

She ran off with the others and I followed them into school, wondering why Angela and Delilah Jones were giggling so much. It was only when I was putting my coat on its peg in the cloakroom that I realized what an idiot I had been. After hanging up their coats all the girls from my class sat down on the benches round the walls and peeled off their coloured

15

tights and leg-warmers, revealing grey school uniform socks underneath.

Angela danced about laughing when she saw my face.

'What a proper Charlie you are, Charlie!' she giggled. 'You fall for it every time!' The other girls gathered round and giggled too, while I stood there in those stupid great red socks feeling like the biggest fool in the whole universe.

Then the second bell rang, and the cloakroom began to empty as most of the girls ran off to the classroom. Jenny Brown came and put her arm round my shoulders, frowning at Angela.

'You are going to give Charlie her socks back now, Angela?' she said severely. 'You promised you would. Otherwise none of us would have agreed to the trick.'

Angela looked indignant. 'Of course I am,' she said, delving into her satchel. 'What do you take me for? It was only a joke.'

Jenny smiled at me and went after the others. I pulled off the red socks and hopped impatiently from one bare foot to the other while Angela rummaged about in her satchel, muttering and shaking her head, and spilling things out onto the floor.

'They're not here, Charlie,' she said at last. 'They must have fallen out somewhere on the way into school.'

I stared at her, aghast.

'What am I going to do?' I squeaked. 'I can't go in with no socks on. Miss Sopwith will kill me!'

Angela smiled that special smile, sweet with something nasty lurking in it, like the medicine Dr Locke gave me when I had the 'flu.

'Sorry, but you'll have to, Charlie,' she said airily. 'It's the red ones or none at all. It's up to you.' And she walked off.

In the end I chose to wear none at all, and I had a hard time explaining to Miss Sopwith, I can tell you. All I could say was that I'd lost them, and I couldn't blame her for not believing me. She gave me a right telling-off, and made me sit with my feet in a cardboard box until Miss Collingwood and her visitors had been round the school.

The other kids felt dead sorry for me, and some of them helped me to look for my socks at playtime. David Watkins found them at last, stuffed behind the bench near the gate, but when I tried to thank him he went all red and embarrassed and wouldn't even look at me. It was something to do with my Valentine card, I felt sure, because I had seen him showing it to the other boys in the corner by the wall. They all burst out laughing when they saw it, and I felt awful when I saw him crumple it up and throw it away in the bin.

I found out why when Laurence Parker nudged my arm on the way back into school.

'That was a brill card you sent to David Watkins,' he chuckled admiringly. 'I didn't know you could be so rude.'

'Rude?' I said, astonished. 'What was rude about it?'

He wouldn't tell me, so I hung back as everybody went inside. I went to the dustbin and retrieved the card, shaking off the toffee papers and crisp crumbs and smoothing out the wrinkles with my hand.

I almost stopped breathing when I read it, for my message had been rubbed out and replaced with another. In Angela's unmistakable careless scrawl, the card now said,

HAPPY VALINTINE'S DAY

FROM THE HART OF MY BOTTOM.

Chapter Two

Angela has had some pretty horrible ideas in her life, but stealing a dog was one of the worst. I thought it was a rotten trick, even if we were short of spending money for the Easter holidays. I would have been quite happy to earn extra cash by running errands and washing dishes, but that didn't suit Angela. Oh no. Not likely. That would be too much like hard work. And if there's one thing Angela can't stand, it's hard work.

We were in my bedroom on a wet windy

day in March, and it was warm and cosy with the radiator on and the rain drumming against the window and one of my mum's soppy old Cliff Richard tapes playing in the corner. I was sitting at my homework table in front of the window, writing a list, and Angela was flat on her back on my bed with her head at the bottom and her brand new expensive Beebop trainers on the pillow.

'What have you got so far, Charlie?' she asked, yawning and shaking her hair back so that it hung over the foot of the bed like a golden curtain.

You wouldn't think anybody so angelic-looking, with such lovely blonde hair and such innocent blue eyes, could possibly get up to the nasty tricks that Angela does. My dad says she's like a poisonous flower, beautiful on the outside and deadly within.

It was only a spelling mistake when I once wrote in my school essay 'Angela Mitchell is my very best *fiend*', but my dad says it suits her perfectly. Mitch the Witch, he calls her, even to her face, but she only grins and blushes as if it's the nicest thing she's ever heard.

I often think I should get rid of Angela and find someone else to play with, but it's not that easy when she lives next door and our mums are such great friends. In any case I've tried going around with other girls lots of times and they all seem so boring compared with her. Every time Angela and I go out together it's like an adventure, and I never know what's going to happen next. And it's not always just me she plays tricks on. We've pulled off some pretty good jokes together as well, like that time we sprayed her dad's daffodils with blue paint, and he thought he had a rare species growing in his garden. So she's not horrible to me all the time. Well, not quite all the time.

Anyway, in reply to her question I put down my pencil and read the title at the top of the list.

'ANGELA MITCHELL AND CHARLOTTE ELLIS – IDEAS FOR EARNING MONEY,' I announced. Then I started reciting all the ideas I'd thought of, and after each one she gave a groan.

'One, washing dishes.'

Groan.

'Two, running errands.'

Groan.

'Three, weeding gardens.'

Groan.

'Four, polishing brass and silver.'

Groan.

'Five, cleaning cars.'

Double groan.

'Six . . .'

'Stop, Charlie, stop,' she begged, covering her face with her hands. 'You can't expect me to do stuff like that.'

I put the list down and sighed. 'You've got to work if you want to earn money,' I pointed out piously, and she snorted through her fingers.

'You sound just like your mum,' she said, and I couldn't help giggling, because she was right.

There was a long silence while I stared at my list and tried to think of things that didn't involve too much effort. But apart from going on the dole I couldn't come up with anything, and I thought we may be a bit young for that. Angela started bicycling her legs in the air, which made my bed creak so much that my dog, Daniel, who had been asleep on the floor underneath, poked his nose out through Angela's curtain of hair to see what was going on. And he looked so funny with Angela's hair hanging down at each side of his face, like a sort of miniature Afghan hound, that I burst out laughing.

Angela sat up and turned round to stare at me.

'I hope you're not laughing at ME, Charlie Ellis,' she said, in her snootiest voice. And it was no use protesting that I wasn't, because by then Daniel's blonde wig wasn't there any more, and he was busy trying to scramble into my lap.

Angela picked up the local paper from my bedside table, where I'd left it after looking in the part-time jobs column, and flung herself down in a huff. I stroked Daniel's ears and waited quietly while she read the paper, because one of the nice things about Angela is that she never sulks for long. Sure enough, after only a couple of minutes she sat up again, grinning like a cat that got the kippers.

'I've got it, Charlie,' she said. 'Listen to this.'

She started to read me something I'd seen earlier, about two boys who had found a lost dog in Edgebourne Park.

'After finding an address on the dog's collar,' she read, 'Roger and Jeremy Dixon took the dog home to its delighted owner, Mrs Louise Featherstone-Browne of Belleview House, Edgebourne. Mrs Featherstone-Browne was so grateful for the return of her beloved pet, a pedigree Airedale terrier called Samantha Twinkletoes, or Sammy for short, that she rewarded the two Dixon boys with twenty pounds each.'

Angela looked up from the paper, her eyes shining. 'Twenty pounds *each*, Charlie,' she said. 'That would buy us a few ice-creams and rides on the dodgems at Fun City. What about that for an idea?'

I sometimes think Angela's not all that bright, even though she's got a devious kind of mind and is always thinking up mischief. There was something fundamentally wrong with this idea of hers, and I told her so.

'To take a lost dog back to its owner . . .' I

said sourly, '. . . you first have to find a lost dog. And where do you think we're going to find a lost dog, Miss Cleverclogs? The park's full of them, I suppose?'

Daniel, who knows the word 'park', had started to jump about and yap in excitement.

'Shut up, Daniel, and let me think,' snapped Angela, and Daniel's tail drooped as he crawled back under the bed.

Angela sat on the edge of the bed with her elbows on her knees and her chin in her hands and I could almost hear her brain ticking. Then a smile began to spread over her face and her eyes went that funny green colour which means she's having one of her fiendish ideas.

'We'll steal one,' she said triumphantly, and my heart turned over in horror at the very thought. 'From somebody really rich, like Mrs Featherbrain What'sername.' She bounced about on the bed. 'Then we'll take it back and get a reward!'

She started capering around my bedroom as if she'd won the pools. 'It's brilliant, Charlie. It can't fail,' she kept saying, tripping over

Daniel who'd rushed out to join her in her capering. And in no time at all it was bedlam, with Daniel barking and dancing around and Angela shouting hooray and whoopee and Cliff Richard warbling on about his 'crying, talking, sleeping, walking, livin' doll.'

The door opened and my mum's face appeared.

'I don't know what's going on in there,' she said, 'but it sounds as if there are twenty kids in that bedroom, not just two. Come on, Angela. Your mum's waiting for you downstairs.'

'Oh, goody,' said Angela. 'She's taking me to buy a new dress. I'll see you later, Charlie. We'll work out a plan.' And she followed my mum down the stairs.

I rushed out onto the landing and shouted down after her.

'You can keep your horrible plan to yourself, Angela Mitchell,' I bellowed. 'I'm having nothing to do with it!'

Then I went back into my room and slammed the door.

The trouble with these schemes of Angela's

is that she never seems to get into trouble. Somehow it's always me that gets the blame. Like the time she moved the ladies' and gents' loo signs from beside the steps of the Portacabins at the Barlow Agricultural Show last September, and swapped them round the wrong way. I didn't think that was a very nice trick, so I picked up the boards and started putting them back where they belonged. Everything would have been all right, only a large lady with arms like a wrestler came out and caught me and thought it was me putting the boards in the wrong place.

I couldn't explain what I was doing without telling tales on Angela, and telling tales would make me almost as bad as she is. So I was grabbed by the scruff of the neck and marched to the gate and chucked out. I had to wait ages for my mum and dad to come out, and when they did I got another good telling-off because of course they had been looking for me all over the show.

So the last thing I wanted to be involved in was stealing a dog. Apart from being unkind to the poor dog, I knew who'd catch it in the neck if we were caught. Angela could just get on with it without me, I told myself, as I turned my pillow over to hide her dirty footprints. Then if anybody got into trouble it would be her.

I didn't see Angela any more that day because she went to tea with her cousin Dominic. And then in the evening my mum and dad and I went to the cinema. It wasn't a very successful evening, because the film turned out to be about elephants being slaughtered by ivory-hunters, which made me watch most of it with my hands over my eyes. Then when we came out my dad went all moody because it had turned frosty and my mum wouldn't let him drive the car.

'The roads look a bit icy, Ted,' she said, getting in on the driver's side. 'You'd better give me the keys.' My mum's a brilliant driver, but since she passed her Advanced Driving Test she thinks she's better than anybody. My dad got into the car without a word, and he didn't speak to either of us all the way home.

Angela turned up the next morning, which was Sunday. The frost had melted and the weather was warm and spring-like, so I thought it would be a good idea to clear out the shed.

I'm very lucky to have my own playshed at the bottom of the garden, where I can be as untidy as I like with nobody telling me it's like a pigsty even if it is. It might not be as posh as Angela's great big playroom, which her dad built specially for her over their garage, but it's quite cosy with pictures and a rug and a cupboard where I can keep all my junk. It's much nicer than Angela's really, because it's away from the house and when I'm there I'm completely by myself. Except for Daniel, that is, who follows me everywhere, even to the loo.

I was filling my rubbish bin with old comics and mouldy apple-cores and Mars Bar wrappers, and Daniel was digging a hole in the rug to look for rabbits which might have strayed into the shed by mistake, when suddenly a voice said, 'Coo-ee!' and Angela appeared in the doorway. She was all dressed up in her best clothes, and she had a fluffy white bundle sticking out of the front of her pink velvet jacket.

'I've done it, Charlie,' she said gleefully, putting the bundle down on the rug next to Daniel. The bundle shook itself and began to yap excitedly as Daniel nudged it with his nose. And my stomach gave the most awful lurch which almost lost me my Sunday morning breakfast of bacon and scrambled eggs and toast.

'It's a dog,' I said stupidly, sitting down in my old wicker armchair which my mum chucked out years ago but which she now wants back because they've become fashionable.

Angela giggled.

'Of course it's a dog, you great twit,' she said. 'I said I'd steal one, didn't I? Well, I have. Cute, isn't it?'

The dog was a white poodle puppy with an unclipped woolly coat and bright dark eyes and I had to admit that it did look cute. It was growling at Daniel and making little runs at him in a sort of mock attack, and Daniel was rolling on his back and kicking his feet in the air, overjoyed to have found a new friend.

'I was hoping I'd find you down here,'

Angela went on blithely. 'Because I'm going to have to leave the puppy with you for a while. I'm off to church now with my mum and dad.'

She bent down and patted the poodle's head. ''Bye for now, doggie,' she cooed. 'We'll take you home to your mummy after church, and your mummy will give us a lovely big reward. 'Bye, Charlie. See you later.'

I was so stunned that for a moment I was speechless. I gulped a couple of times, then my voice came back at last.

'Hey, hang on . . .!' I managed to protest, as she went out of the door. 'You're not leaving that dog here. I've told you I'm having nothing to do with this stupid plan of yours.'

She turned to look at me, with that disgusted expression that makes you feel like crawling into a cupboard and never coming out.

'What else can I do, Charlie?' she demanded, hands on hips. 'I can hardly take it to church with me, can I?'

Even I could see the truth of that. And even though I didn't like the idea one bit, I didn't see how I could refuse.

'Go on, Charlie,' she wheedled. 'It'll only be

for an hour or so. Then we'll take the puppy home and say we found it.'

She stood there smiling at me but I didn't feel in the least like smiling back. I felt more like tipping the binful of rubbish over her head. I gave a long-suffering sigh, like my mum does when my dad goes to the pub with Uncle Jim for a pint of beer.

'Just for an hour, then,' I muttered reluctantly. 'Just until you get back from church.'

She laughed and went skipping off, delighted to be getting her own way as usual.

'But I'm *not* coming with you to take it back,' I shouted after her. 'And that's final!'

She turned and waved, and then she disappeared round the corner.

The stinking rotten cat, I thought to myself. She'll be sitting there in church looking all sweet and angelic, singing about God's creatures great and small, when all the time she's a dog-thief. She mustn't have a scrap of conscience, I decided. If she really believed in God she wouldn't dare even go to church.

I sat there wondering why I'm such a wimp when it comes to dealing with Angela, and wishing I was brave enough to stick up for myself a bit more. Then after a while the puppy came and put its front paws on my knees and looked up at me with its head on one side, and I suddenly had the feeling that I'd seen it before. And very recently too.

'Miss Menzies!' I exclaimed, picking up the astonished puppy and giving it a squeeze. 'You belong to Miss Menzies, just down the road. Angela hasn't stolen you at all!'

Miss Menzies is an enormous lady with orange hair who sings in the Barlow Opera Company and eats cream cakes all the time when she's not singing, and sometimes even when she is. She's so huge my dad says she could get a job in a circus, see-sawing with an elephant. Angela's mum and Miss Menzies are friends, so I knew it would have been dead easy for Angela to borrow the dog, pretending she was taking it for a walk.

What a slyboots she is, I said to myself. It's just one of her tricks. She only said she'd stolen the puppy to give me a fright. She's always doing that sort of thing. Like that day when she pretended she'd kidnapped a baby, and it was only her little cousin all the time.

The puppy wasn't wearing a collar, so there was no clue there, but the more I looked at it the more convinced I was that I was right. So without wasting any more time I stuffed the puppy into the top of my anorak and set off with it up the garden path to the gate.

Daniel trotted along beside me, and down the road we went, past Angela's house where there was no car in the drive because they were all still at church, past the new white bungalows called Costa Brava and Costa Del Sol, which my dad says should be called Costa Packet and Costa Narm Andaleg, and then we were at Miss Menzies' shiny red-painted gate, where I remembered seeing a white poodle puppy only a few days before, peeping out at me with its head on one side.

That's fixed you, Angela Mitchell, I giggled to myself, as I leaned over the gate and put the puppy down on the ground just inside. That'll show you I'm not as stupid as you think. And Daniel and I hopscotched happily all the way home.

I was shaking the rug outside the shed door, and Daniel was trying to get his teeth in the corner to start a game of tug o'war, when Angela turned up, back from church. Her face was all pale and tragic, and her cheeks were streaked with what looked like tears.

'Charlie!' she cried, flinging herself into my arms. 'I've been thinking all through the service. What a terrible, wicked thing I did this morning, stealing that poor dog!'

I laughed and pushed her away from me. 'Come off it, Angela,' I snorted. 'I'm not as green as I'm cabbage-looking. You didn't steal any dog. You're only having me on.'

'Oh, Charlie. I only wish I was,' she gulped, scrubbing her eyes with her hanky. 'But I really did steal it. From outside the paper shop when I went to get my dad's *Sunday Times*. But now I'm really, really sorry. The owners must be worried out of their minds by now.'

She clutched my arm and gave a little sob. 'You will come with me to take it home, Charlie, won't you? Please? I promise I won't let them give us a reward.'

'I've already taken it home,' I told her smugly. 'I put it in Miss Menzies' garden more than half an hour ago. So you can just stick that in your pipe and smoke it, Angela Mitchell!'

I started banging the rug against the corner of the shed, but Angela pulled me round to face her.

'MISS MENZIES?' she shrieked. 'You idiot, Charlie! It's not Miss Menzies' dog. Miss Menzies' dog is a GIRL. The one I left with you was a BOY!'

I stared at her and I knew by her face that this time she was telling the truth, although I don't know how she could tell the difference, with a puppy as woolly as an unclipped poodle.

'Oh,' I said, and I felt a proper fool, I can tell you.

Angela started to pull me up the garden. 'Come on, Charlie!' she urged. 'We've got to get that dog back before Miss Menzies finds it and reports it to the police!'

I could see the sense of that, so I hurried with her back down the road. Daniel scampered along, tail waving like a banner. This is great, he seemed to be saying. What a lot of walkies we're having today!

I got a shock when we arrived at Miss Menzies' gate, for racing happily round the garden were, not one white poodle puppy, but two. They were having the time of their lives, galloping through the flowerbeds, flattening the crocuses and trampling the new green shoots on the daffodils.

'Good grief,' I said. 'There's two of them.'

'Quick, Charlie. Grab him!' said Angela, opening the gate. But for one thing the puppies were having such a great time that they didn't want to be grabbed, and for another I didn't know which one to grab even if they did. Daniel rushed in to join the fun, and soon we were all charging round the garden like stampeding bullocks in a western on the telly.

'Good gracious! Whatever's going on?' cried a horrified voice, and there on the front doorstep stood Miss Menzies, in a huge purple jogging suit that would have been a good fit on a hippopotamus.

We all froze like statues, even the dogs. Angela and I looked at one another helplessly, each hoping the other would think of something to say. Then one of the puppies ran to

Miss Menzies and jumped up at her, wagging its tail.

'Come to Mummy, darling,' cooed Miss Menzies, scooping it up into her arms.

Angela at once grabbed the other puppy and headed for the gate. I dithered for a moment, opening and shutting my mouth like a singer on the telly with the sound turned off, until the sight of Miss Menzies bearing down on me as angry as an alligator brought me to life.

'Come on, Daniel,' I said, and we all scooted out of the gate and up the road.

I didn't stop running until we reached our back door. I paused for a moment to push Daniel safely into the house, while Angela ran straight down to the playshed. When I got there she had flopped down into my chair and the puppy was playing on the floor.

'Phew! That was a close one!' she puffed, delving into the pocket of her jacket. 'Now we'll see where this dog really belongs. The sooner we get him home the better.'

She produced a thin leather dog-lead, and a midget-sized collar with one of those little tubes that hold the dog's name and address.

'I took his collar off him earlier on,' she explained, unscrewing the tiny cap on the tube and teasing out the scrap of paper inside. 'I haven't had a chance to look at this yet.' She peered closely at the name and address, frowning.

'It's teeny writing,' she complained. 'Miss Call . . . something, I think. You have a look, Charlie. I can't make it out.'

I went to the window where the sunshine was streaming in. I held the paper up to the light and read the name and address written on it. Then I felt an icy chill all over, like you get when you're standing in the shower and the water suddenly turns cold.

'Miss COLLINGWOOD!' I yelped, as if somebody had trodden on my foot. 'It says MISS COLLINGWOOD, THREE WILLOW DRIVE, EDGEBOURNE!' I dropped the paper hurriedly into Angela's lap. 'You've REALLY done it this time, Angela Mitchell,' I shouted at her. 'You've stolen the HEADMISTRESS'S DOG!'

Angela clutched at the arms of the chair with both hands and I could see that she was about to have hysterics. Miss Collingwood is a kind and fair headmistress, but there are three things that make her go really wild. Swearing is one of them, lying is another, and unkindness to animals is the third. I had a feeling that Angela wouldn't be half so keen to take the dog back now that she knew whose it was.

I was right. Angela put her hanky over her face and started wailing and throwing herself about, the way she did when I won the Edgebourne Arts Society Children's Painting Competition instead of her.

'I can't do it,' she cried, twisting her hanky as if she was wringing out the dishcloth. 'I can't tell Miss Collingwood I found the puppy. She'll know it's a lie.' She flung herself on the floor at my feet and wrapped her arms round my knees. 'You take him back, Charlie,' she begged. 'I know she'll believe you!'

That was the last straw. I might be a bit soft but I'm not altogether brainless. I shot out of that shed as if it was about to blow up, and scarpered up the path towards the house.

Angela's wails followed me up the garden, but I ignored them. She got herself into this mess, I told myself. She can just get herself out of it. It's nothing to do with me.

I had almost reached the kitchen door when I bumped into Auntie Sally coming down the path, wobbling along the crazy paving in her high-heeled shoes. She's not my real aunt, but I'm allowed to call her that because she's Angela's mum.

'Whoops! Careful, Charlie!' she laughed. 'I'm just coming to look for Angela. We're having an early lunch today. We're going to Barlow to have tea with Angela's Auntie Beth and Uncle Peter.'

I said a very rude word under my breath. 'She's down in the shed,' I scowled, clenching my fists in my pockets. 'Having hysterics,' I added spitefully. But Auntie Sally wasn't listening. She was looking past my shoulder and beaming all over her face.

'Angela, there you are!' she said. 'Come along, darling. Lunch is ready. We must be off in half an hour.'

'I was just coming, Mum,' said Angela, trotting through the rhubarb patch.

And she went sailing past me as if nothing

had happened and stolen dogs were just something you heard about on the telly. She'd cleaned up her face and there were no signs of hysterics, so she must have switched them off as quickly as she'd switched them on. Even Angela has learnt that hysterics are not worth all the bother unless you've got an audience to impress.

Angela's mum tripped away up the drive, and Angela turned and hissed into my ear. 'Now you'll just have to take the puppy back yourself, Charlie. Otherwise you'll have to keep the poor thing all day. I'll ring you this evening to find out what happened.'

She ran after her mum and linked arms with her. 'What's for lunch, Mum?' she said. 'I'm starving.'

And off they went together, chatting about roast beef and Yorkshire pudding and peach trifle and cream, while I stood there kicking the trunk of the apple tree and wishing it was Angela's head.

I stopped after a minute or two because it was making an awful mess of my new Strike trainers, and anyway it wasn't the apple tree's fault if Angela was a rotten toad. I went back down to the shed and opened the door, and when I saw the puppy sitting there all by himself with his big eyes looking so sad and lonely I knew that the only thing I could do was take him home. I really had no choice. I had to do it, not just for the poor dog's sake, but for Miss Collingwood's, too. She must be frantic with worry by now, and it wasn't fair.

I looked at my watch and found it was just after twelve, so there was plenty of time to get to Willow Drive and back before lunch at one. Angela had left the collar and lead on the chair, so I put them in my pocket, stuffed the puppy once more into the front of my anorak and hurried up the garden and into the street.

As soon as we were out of our neighbourhood I put the puppy on the ground and put his collar and lead on him. It hardly mattered if anybody saw me with him now, so he might as well have some exercise. He bounced along, sniffing at everything he saw, and watering every lamp-post within reach.

It would have been a nice walk but my heart was thumping too much for me to enjoy it. All the way along the road and through the town and over the bridge and along the river bank towards the posh private estate called Abbotsford where Miss Collingwood lives I rehearsed in my head what I was going to say. I didn't want to tell tales on Angela, but knowing how Miss Collingwood feels about telling lies I knew I couldn't make up any kind of story. All I could hope was that she would just take it for granted that I'd found the dog. Maybe she would be so pleased to get him back she wouldn't ask any awkward questions. And maybe if I was really fortunate I could just bundle the dog into the garden without her seeing me at all.

No such luck. I could see Miss Collingwood in her front garden as soon as I turned the corner into Willow Drive. She was chatting to a neighbour over the hedge, and she had a trowel in one hand and a bucket in the other, as if she had been doing some gardening.

Gardening! When her dog had been missing for over two hours! I always get in a panic if Daniel goes missing for more than five minutes. She mustn't care about her poor dog one bit, I told myself crossly. I'd been getting all steamed up for nothing.

Miss Collingwood waved her trowel and beamed at me when she saw me coming round the corner. She said something to the neighbour, then came towards me and opened the front gate. The puppy jumped up at her and put his muddy paws on her skirt, but she only laughed and patted his head, so I suppose it must have been an old gardening skirt which didn't matter.

'Hello, Muffin,' she said to the puppy. 'Did you have a lovely time? You have had a nice long walk!'

She took the lead from me and smiled. 'Hello, Charlie. Thanks for bringing Muffin back. Angela said you might. She had to go to Barlow or somewhere, didn't she?'

Miss Collingwood put her hand in the pocket of her baggy Arran cardigan that looked as if it came from the Senior Citizens' jumble sale, and took out a small purse.

'Fifty pence an hour for dog-walking, I think Angela said?' She glanced at her watch and started doing some sums in her head. 'Now,

46

let's see. Angela collected Muffin at about nine-thirty. We'll call it three hours, shall we? I must say I think it's commendable of Angela to want to earn money for the Easter holidays. Especially since her father lost his job like that. Most commendable indeed.'

She put a pound coin and a fifty-pence piece into my limp hand and closed my fingers round it. 'Give this to Angela, will you, Charlie?' she said. 'And do say thank you to her for me. It gave me a chance to catch up on the weeding, without having to keep an eye on Muffin all the time. I'm really most grateful.'

I managed to pull myself together and totter out of the gate. Miss Collingwood must have thought I was a real dimwit, because I couldn't even bring myself to say thank you or even goodbye. As soon as I was in the street I ran like the wind for home, with Miss Collingwood's one pound fifty burning a hole in my hand.

The paper shop was still open as I went past, and I suddenly thought of something. I went in and dropped the coins into the RSPCA collecting box on the counter.

'Thank you, Charlie,' said Mr Kinnear the newsagent, with an astonished smile that made his moustache bend up at the corners. 'That's very generous. That must have been a whole week's pocket money.'

I grinned weakly and scuttled out. Some homeless dog somewhere might as well get the benefit of it, I thought. And I felt a lot better about the whole thing.

Angela never did believe me when I told her what I'd done with the money, though. When she rang me later that evening to giggle and gloat about the way she'd tricked me and to claim her share of the loot, she had the nerve to accuse me of keeping it all for myself. She really is the absolute pig's limit sometimes.

Chapter Three

I've never been so scared as I was that day with Angela in Jason's Wood. Not even when I thought we'd poisoned Laurence Parker with deadly nightshade in the garden last summer and he collapsed in a heap in the rhubarb patch. That was pretty scary, but what we thought we'd found in Jason's Wood was ten times worse.

It happened during our half-term holiday back in February, on a freezing cold Monday morning when spring had suddenly turned back into winter. My mum and dad and I had been to Northumberland to stay with my gran for the weekend, and it had started to snow as we were driving home on Sunday afternoon. By the time we reached Edgebourne the roads and hedges were already turning white, and big flakes were dashing themselves at the head-lights as my mum turned the car into our drive.

'They're playing suitable music, anyway,' she said, switching off the engine and the car radio at the same time. 'That was the London Chamber Orchestra playing Winter, from the Four Seasons by Vivaldi.'

My mum's been doing an Open University course on classical music, and she doesn't half like to show off.

'What's a chamber orchestra?' I said, getting out of the car with a sleepy Daniel in my arms.

'They all sit on their potties to play,' said my dad, and my mum snorted disapprovingly while my dad roared with laughter.

We unloaded the luggage and struggled up the slippery path to the front door.

'It looks as if it's going to snow all night,'

said my dad, slamming the door against the blizzard. 'My toes feel like ten frozen fish fingers. Turn the heating up a bit, Charlie hinny.'

My dad always calls me Charlie hinny when we've been staying with my gran because that's what she calls me. In fact she calls everybody hinny. She calls my dad Ted hinny and my mum Liz hinny and my dog Daniel hinny and my grandad Joe hinny and it does sound funny. She's got a neighbour called Winnie, and when she calls her hinny it sounds funnier still.

'Fish don't have fingers, Dad,' I said, but I turned the thermostat up in the hall, thinking how lucky we are to have a nice warm house instead of an igloo at the North Pole or a tent in Siberia.

When I woke up on Monday morning and looked out of the window I was glad it was a school holiday, because the sun was shining and the world was snuggling under a big white duvet of snow. I scrambled out of bed and put on my jeans and my warmest sweater.

'Come on, Daniel,' I said. 'Let's go out and build a snowdog.'

Daniel thought that was a brilliant idea and we galloped downstairs. My mum was in the kitchen watching the news on the portable telly she keeps on the worktop so she doesn't have to miss her Open University programme when she's peeling the potatoes.

'Nothing but weather on the news this morning,' she said, switching off the telly and stirring something in a saucepan on the stove. 'There's chaos on the roads. Your dad's taking the morning off work.'

I peered into the pan to see what she was cooking. 'Can I go out to play in the garden?' I said. 'Daniel and me want to make a snowdog.'

'Daniel and I,' corrected my mum with a frown. 'And you can go when you've got a hot breakfast inside you.' She spooned a dollop of porridge into a plate and put it on the table.

I sprinkled it with sugar and poured on some cream. I was just about to take the first delicious mouthful when the phone rang in the hall. It was Angela.

'Hi, Charlie,' she said. 'Isn't this brill! Shall I come round? We could build a snowman.'

I said I was just about to have breakfast and she could come round in ten minutes. Then just before she hung up she suddenly changed her mind.

'Oh, hang on, Charlie,' she said. 'I've just remembered there's something I have to do. I'll be round in about an hour. Right?'

'All right,' I said, and went back to my porridge. When I'd finished I put my anorak on, the quilted one with the furry hood.

'Charlie,' said my mum. 'If you're going out, get well wrapped up. And tell your dad to come in for his breakfast before it gets cold.'

I hate the way grown-ups tell you to get well wrapped up, as if you were a parcel for the post, but I put on my scarf and my gloves and my woolly hat and my wellies, and Daniel and I went outside.

My dad stopped shovelling snow when he saw us and threw a snowball at Daniel. Daniel jumped up to catch it in his mouth, but missed.

'Butterteeth!' laughed my dad.

I gave him my mum's message and he went inside.

While Daniel raced about barking at the snow and digging holes in it and chasing imaginary arctic hares, I built the biggest snowdog you've ever seen. It had pointed ears, pebbles for its eyes, and a lump of shiny black coal for its nose.

Angela fell about laughing when she came round the corner and saw it.

'That's great, Charlie,' she said. 'It looks just like Bonzo, my Uncle Jack's doberman.'

I grinned at her. Her face was flushed and excited, and she was breathing quickly as if she had run a long way.

'You shouldn't say dober*man* any more,' I told her. 'It's sexist. You should say dober*person*. Like chairperson. My dad said so.'

She snorted in disgust and started throwing snowballs at Daniel, while I got an old scarf out of the box in the shed and tied it round the snowdog's neck. Finally I stuck a clay pipe into its mouth and stood back to admire the effect.

'There,' I said. 'It really is a doberperson now.'

Angela collected some more bits of coal from

around the coal bunker and pressed them into the snowdog so that it had black spots all over.

'It's not a doberperson now, Charlie. It's a damnation,' she said, dead pleased with herself.

'You mean dalmation,' I giggled, but Angela had lost interest.

'Let's go for a walk now,' she said. 'It'll be magic in Lane End Beeches.'

'OK,' I replied. 'But I'll have to tell my mum first. And I'll have to get Daniel's lead.'

My mum had her nose in a seed catalogue when I opened the kitchen door.

'Chuck me Daniel's lead, will you please, Mum?' I said. 'Angela and me are taking him for a walk in Lane End Beeches.'

'Angela and I,' said my mum absently, but she got the lead down from its hook and threw it towards the door.

We set off towards Barlow, where lorries were out putting grit on the roads. Snow scrunched under our boots, our breaths came out in puffs of steam, and Hawthorn Hill was like a Christmas card, with snow-covered trees and kids in brightly-coloured clothes sledging on the slopes towards the river.

'Come on, Charlie,' Angela kept saying impatiently. 'What are you dawdling about for? I thought we were going for a walk.'

'What's the hurry?' I grumbled, but I let myself be hurried along.

We passed the phone box on the main road and turned down the track into Lane End Beeches. Snow lay deep on the path and in drifts against the hedge, and walking was quite hard work. Daniel kept sinking in up to his middle, and he sometimes had to take great leaps and bounds to make any progress at all.

'Angela,' I said suddenly. 'There's been somebody along here already this morning.'

I'd just noticed some footprints in the snow going in the same direction as ours. Then almost immediately I spotted a similar line of prints pointing the other way.

'Look, there's the same prints going back again,' I said. 'And it must have been someone about our age, too. The footprints are the same size as ours.'

'Maybe it was a woozle,' giggled Angela,

and I giggled too, remembering the story about Piglet and Winnie-the-Pooh.

Daniel bounded on ahead, sniffing at the lovely woody smells and barking to tell those rabbits and foxes and badgers that he was on his way to sort them all out. Then suddenly he pounced on something half-buried in the snow under a holly bush. He dragged it out and started to worry it and growl and stick his bottom in the air and wag his tail.

'What's Daniel found?' said Angela. 'It looks like a hat.'

'Daniel, fetch!' I commanded. And, like the good, well-trained dog he is, he brought the thing straight to me and sat down with it in his mouth.

'Good boy!' I said, taking the object from him and turning it over in my hand.

It was a man's hat, a sort of brown tweedy one, and it couldn't have been there long because it was still clean and respectable, apart from being a bit wet from the snow.

'Somebody must have lost it,' I said, folding it and starting to put it into my anorak pocket. 'I'll hand it in at the post office on the way home.'

But Angela had snatched the hat from me

and was staring at it as if she'd never seen a hat in her life.

'Charlie,' she breathed. 'It's a brown tweed hat. That old man who went missing had a brown tweed hat. I wonder if it's his.'

'What old man?' I said, and she gave me a tragic look from those huge blue eyes.

'Oh, Charlie, didn't you know?' she said. 'Some poor old man from Edgebourne went missing on Saturday. It was on the local telly while you were away.'

She gazed apprehensively at the hat as if it were about to leap up and bite her.

'He went out for a walk and nobody has seen him since,' she went on. 'They said he had a brown tweed hat, and a walking stick, and red knitted gloves . . .'

She clutched my arm. 'Ooh, Charlie, you don't think . . .?'

The sun went behind a cloud and the beech trees looked suddenly menacing in the gloom. I shivered, and wished I was at home in our nice warm kitchen.

'Don't be silly, Angela,' I said. 'If he only got lost in the woods surely they'd have found him by now. They would have had dogs out and everything.'

Angela didn't look convinced. She stuffed the hat in her pocket and we went on, casting sideways glances at every clump of bushes or drift of snow.

It was a walking stick we found next. It was leaning against a tree, and I would have walked straight past it if Angela hadn't spotted it and darted forward. She held it out to show me and I shivered again.

'This must be his walking stick,' she gulped. 'He must be here somewhere, Charlie.'

'Let's go home,' I said hurriedly. 'We'll tell somebody what we've found . . .'

But Angela wasn't having any of that.

'We can't do that,' she argued. 'He could be lying ill or injured or . . . or . . . something. We can't just go off and leave him.'

She began to poke about in the snowdrifts with the walking stick. 'You can do what you like, Charlie Ellis,' she said. 'But I'm going to have a good look round.'

So of course there was nothing for me to do but help.

A few light flakes had started to fall as she spoke, and the sky had turned that ominous dirty-yellow colour which means more snow. We trudged along, prodding every hummock and ditch for any tell-tale signs, while the snow fell faster and faster round us and Daniel danced about trying to catch it in his mouth.

The track came to an end near the gate into Jason's Wood. We could go no further without trespassing on private land.

'Well, that's it,' I said. 'Come on, Angela. We'll have to go back now.'

I started back the way we had come, but Angela gave a sudden cry that stopped me in my tracks. I turned again to see her gazing over the gate at a clump of brambles just inside the wood. Her expression was so horrified that I had to go back and see what she was looking at.

I plodded to her side and peered over the gate. And that's when I saw it. Something that made my knees buckle under me as if I'd been kicked from behind.

It was a red glove, sticking stiffly out from a snowdrift under the brambles, as if someone was buried there and was trying to crawl out.

We clung together, breathing hard. The snow went on falling around us.

'Crumbs. It's him,' whispered Angela, round-eyed. 'Climb over the gate, Charlie. Try giving him artificial perspiration.'

'Not blooming likely,' I croaked. 'You go. You're the one who found him.'

'Ooh, Charlie. I just daren't,' said Angela. 'What are we going to do?'

'We'll get help,' I said promptly. 'There's a call box at the end of the lane. I'll run and phone my dad. He'll know what to do.'

'We can't both go,' objected Angela, shuddering as if she'd been sitting in the freezer with no clothes on. 'One of us will have to phone, and the other will have to stay here and keep guard.'

I took another look at that red glove sticking out from the snow and I knew which I'd rather do.

'You stay here,' I said quickly. 'I'll go to the phone. I can run faster than you anyway.'

And before she could do anything to stop me I plunged away up the lane.

I couldn't run properly because of the snow

61

so it took me quite a while to reach the main road. Daniel scampered beside me as I struggled along, and it was comforting to have him with me. At least he was enjoying himself, I thought, even if nobody else was.

The phone box came in sight at last but when I got there somebody was in it. Three teenage girls in purple and green and orange shell-suits and panda eye make-up, all squashed into the phone box together. They must have been ringing up their boyfriends or something because they kept passing the receiver back and forth and giggling and saying, 'Ooh, what a thing to say.' They put their tongues out at me and thumbed their noses when I banged on the glass and shouted at them that I needed to make an urgent call.

They came out at last, sniggering and pushing one another and fooling about, and they looked me up and down as if I was something that fell off the moon. I took no notice of them, and slipped into the phone box, pulling Daniel in after me and shutting the door.

My hands were shaking so much that I could hardly dial the number. And I don't think I've ever been so pleased to hear my dad's voice.

'Oh Dad. It's me,' I quavered thankfully. Then I blurted out the story.

My dad listened without interrupting while I described how Angela and I had found the hat, and the walking stick, and the red-gloved hand sticking out of the snow. When he spoke his voice sounded grim.

'It sounds like one of Angela's stupid pranks to me,' he said. 'I heard the local news this morning on the radio, and there was nothing about any missing old man. But wait there, Charlie. I'll be along in two minutes. Just to make sure.'

He hung up.

I stamped my frozen feet to warm them while I waited at the end of the lane, and I thought about what my dad had said. If somebody had really gone missing from Edgebourne, then surely it would have been on the local news. And surely my mum would have seen it on the telly.

Then I remembered the first set of footprints. I remembered that *somebody else* had been down the lane already that morning. I hunted around until I found the prints again, half-buried under fresh snow.

Angela's footprints of course.

And when I thought it all over I had a funny feeling I wasn't going to find Angela hanging around when I got back to Jason's Wood.

I was right. My dad's car pulled into the kerb a few minutes later and my dad jumped out. He gave me a quick hug and then we trudged together down the lane. And when we reached the gate Angela had disappeared.

Not only was there no Angela, but there was no hat, no walking stick, and no red-gloved hand. Only fresh prints going away through the wood showed that Angela must have climbed the gate, walked through Jason's Wood even though it private, and slipped off home another way.

My dad had a good poke about, but what had looked so much like a body before was now only a mound of snow. I couldn't help feeling relieved, but my dad was hopping mad. He stomped off up the lane to the car, muttering darkly about what he was going to say to that little minx the next time he caught up with her. And Daniel and I hurried after him, vowing we'd never be friends with her again.

My dad calmed down after hot chicken soup and toasted cheese sandwiches for lunch. He told my mum all about what had happened, making it sound really funny, and before long they were both laughing and saying what a kid and whatever will she think of next.

After lunch my dad went off to work. My mum and I were washing up in the kitchen when who should come dancing past the window but Angela, grinning all over her face and wearing the brown tweed hat, which must have been her dad's all the time. In one hand she was swinging the walking stick, like Fred Astaire in an old film on the telly, and in the other she was waving a bit of garden cane, with a stuffed red glove stuck on the end of it.

I pulled the curtain across so I wouldn't have to look at her, but my mum peered out and smiled.

'She's a proper little rascal, isn't she?' she said admiringly.

'She's a pain in the bottom,' I said sourly. 'I'm not playing with her any more. She's always causing trouble for Daniel and I.' And I put a little stress on the 'I', to show that I could get it right for once.

'Daniel and *me*,' corrected my mum, shaking her head impatiently, and I heaved an enormous sigh.

I wish they'd make their minds up sometimes. I really do.

Chapter Four

Idanced along the landing towards the bath-room one spring morning, when the sun was streaming in through the hall window and you could hear the sparrows cheeping their feathers off in the garden outside.

'I'm going to the loo, loo, loo,' I sang. 'How about you, you, you? I'm gonna do a . . .'

'That's quite enough, Charlotte,' snapped my mum, coming out of the bathroom with a towel round her head. 'You don't have to be so disgusting.'

'Dad sings it,' I said. 'I heard him singing it yesterday.'

'Your dad should know better,' frowned my mum, tutting as she shut her bedroom door.

I sat on the loo, trying to work out why it's always the dads who think jokes about lavatories and bottoms are funny and always the mums who frown and tut and say how rude, and wondering how soon it would be before I started getting more like my mum and less like my dad. But it was too nice a morning to worry about things like that. I washed and dressed quickly and danced down the stairs.

'I'm a troll, fol-de-rol, I'm a troll, fol-de-rol,' I sang, because it was safer, and Daniel came rushing out of his basket to growl and attack my slippers, which is what he always does whenever I dance or sing.

'You sound like an exceedingly droll troll,' said my dad, making toast in the kitchen. 'Why are you so happy today?'

'No special reason,' I said, sitting down at the table. 'It's just a nice day. And it's Saturday and there's no school. And I did all my homework last night. So for the rest of the weekend I can do exactly as I please.'

My mum came in with a basket of dirty washing. 'Lucky you,' she said grumpily. 'I wish I could do exactly as I please for the weekend, instead of having to make the beds, do the washing, clean the windows, do the shopping, cook the lunch, do the ironing, cook the supper, feed the dog . . .'

'Poor old Bizzie Lizzie,' said my dad. 'All I have to do is cook the breakfast, wash the dishes, clean the car, mow the lawn, wash the dishes, dig the garden, clip the hedge, put up shelves, wash the dishes, chop the wood, feed the dog . . .'

'You don't both have to feed the dog,' I pointed out, and they looked at one another and burst out laughing.

'No wonder Daniel's getting so fat,' said my dad, and he put a handful of Crunchy Bites into Daniel's bowl.

'He's not the only one,' retorted my mum, bundling the washing into the machine, and my dad made a face behind her back.

I knew they were only joking, but all the

same I couldn't help feeling a bit guilty when I thought about the piles of chores they had to do, when I had none at all. I buttered some toast and spread it with honey, wondering what I could do to help.

'Couldn't I do the shopping, Mum?' I offered, after a minute. 'That would save you a bit of time.'

My mum put some washing powder in the machine and switched it on.

'That's nice of you, poppet. But you'd never carry a whole week's groceries. I'll have to take the car to the supermarket.'

I thought about it some more.

'If we made a list,' I said, 'I could walk down to the supermarket and fill a trolley up with all the stuff. I could wait in the car park with the loaded trolley. Then all you have to do is drive down, put the shopping in the car, and drive home again. It would only take you ten minutes.'

My mum stared at me. Then she looked at my dad.

'What do you think, Ted?' she said. 'Do you think we should let her?'

'I think it's a great idea,' said my dad. 'She can't come to any harm in the supermarket.'

My mum still didn't look very sure. 'I'm not happy about letting you go on your own,' she told me. 'Give Angela a ring and see if she'll go with you.'

I licked my fingers so I wouldn't put honey all over the phone as my mum doesn't like her hair getting glued to the receiver. Then I dialled Angela's number, and Angela answered.

'Edgebourne five-oh-five-oh-twoooo?' she warbled, in the posh voice she and Auntie Sally always use on the phone, in case they get a call from the Queen or Cilla Black.

She listened while I told her the plan. 'That's brilliant,' she said, when I'd finished. 'How much are they giving you?'

'I'm not doing it for money,' I said virtuously. 'I'm doing it to help my mum.'

'More fool you,' said Angela. 'I thought we were supposed to be earning some pocket money for the holidays.'

'Not from our own parents. That's stupid,' I said, and then I wished I hadn't, because she went all huffy on me at once.

71

'Are you calling me stupid, Charlie Ellis?' she demanded. 'Because if you are . . .'

'No, of course not,' I said hastily. 'I only meant . . . it's just that . . .' I suddenly got fed up with arguing about it. 'Look, Angela,' I said. 'Are you coming or not? If you're not, just say so. I'll ring Jane McLachlan and ask her.'

'Oh, I'll come,' said Angela. 'I'll do my mum's shopping as well. But I'm not doing it for nothing. I'll tell her it's worth at least a quid.'

I went back to the table with some paper and a pen.

'Angela's going to do her mum's shopping too,' I said. 'Right, Mum? You dictate. I'll write it down.' My mum started reeling off items one after the other, and by the time she'd finished I'd covered both sides of the paper.

Angela came skipping down the drive a little while later, and she had her brown cord trousers on and that brown and yellow stripy jumper that her Auntie Beth brought her from Canada.

'Here's Angela,' said my mum, looking out of the window. 'She's wearing that lovely jumper. The one that makes her look like a little bee.'

'Angela *is* a little B,' said my dad, and my mum tutted like anything and said, 'Ted, how could you say such a thing.'

I zipped my mum's money safely away in a deep pocket in my anorak and kissed a doleful Daniel on the nose.

'I'll pick you and Angela up at eleven-thirty,' said my mum. 'That should give you plenty of time.'

Angela and I set off together along the street towards Edgebourne, which isn't really a village and isn't really a town but more like something in between, with a newly-built supermarket and car park in the middle of the High Street where the old village post office used to be. We went down the main road and along Walton Terrace where there are no front gardens, and where a row of empty milk bottles stood on the doorsteps next to the pavement awaiting the milkman's arrival.

'I hope you're going to behave yourself for

once,' I said to Angela as we went along. 'I don't want you getting me into any trouble in the supermarket.'

She laughed and tossed her hair. 'Trouble? Me?' she snorted, as if she'd never caused trouble in her life. Then she bent down to one of the doorsteps where somebody had left out one of those little wooden indicator boards that tell the milkman if you want extra milk. The arrow on the dial was pointing to two extra pints, and it only took Angela a couple of seconds to reset it.

'That'll give somebody a surprise,' she giggled, turning the arrow right round to fourteen. Then she went racing off, laughing and throwing her purse in the air, leaving me to hurry along behind, casting anxious glances over my shoulder in case anybody was looking.

Inside the supermarket it wasn't so bad. It was still fairly early in the morning so there weren't too many people about, and apart from ramming a few people in the behind with her trolley, and getting into an argument with an assistant because she couldn't find any

Mucousade or Muggle-a-Tony soup, she managed to get round most of the aisles without too much bother. I thankfully got on with my own shopping, filling the trolley with butter and bacon and eggs and cheese and sausages and pizzas and lettuces and apples and broccoli and washing-up liquid and shoe-polish and Meaty Chunks.

We went through two adjacent check-outs, grinning and putting our tongues out at one another across the tills as we packed all the stuff into plastic carrier bags and paid for it. Then we loaded the bags back into the trolleys and wheeled them towards the door.

The smell of hot doughnuts and coffee hit our noses as we went past the supermarket cafeteria, and my stomach rumbled in response. Angela looked at her watch.

'It's only eleven o'clock, Charlie,' she said. 'We've got half an hour to wait. Shall we have a doughnut or a Kit-Kat or something?'

I shook my head. 'No money,' I said ruefully. 'I've put all my pocket money in my piggy bank for the holidays.'

'I'll pay,' said Angela generously. One good

thing about Angela is that she's never mean with her money. 'My mum gave me two pounds for doing the shopping,' she added. And she pushed her trolley through the café doors.

It's a tiny cafeteria with only half a dozen tables, and by now the place was beginning to get busy. At first I thought we weren't going to find a table, then Angela nudged my arm.

'Over there,' she said. 'There's two seats beside Evil Edna.'

Evil Edna is really called Edna Eevle and she's a librarian. All the kids call her Evil Edna because she's got a long sour face like a stick of rhubarb from scowling so much and what she hates most in the world is unruly children coming into her nice clean tidy library. And she's not only sour but greedy too. If she sees you with sweets or crisps she confiscates them and eats them herself, and she's always throwing you out for making a noise or mucking about or playing hide and seek behind the bookcases. I once got chucked out for sneezing, which wasn't fair because Angela had just sprinkled pepper inside a book and slammed it shut in front of my nose.

'We don't want to sit next to her,' I said. 'She's horrible. She's got a face like a Hallowe'en mask. My dad says she's so ugly she could haunt houses.'

'Oh, come on,' said Angela impatiently. 'There's no other seats. And besides, we might be able to have some fun with her.'

She parked her trolley next to Evil Edna's table, so there was nothing for it but to do the same, although I felt a bit glum. Angela's idea of having fun with somebody in a café is to kick them on the shin under the table and then say it was me.

'You stay here and keep the seats, Charlie,' said Angela. 'I'll get you a doughnut. The coffee's foul because they make it with paralysed milk. Shall we have coke?'

'Yes, please,' I said, and Angela went to the self-service counter and started loading a tray.

I sat down, eyeing Evil Edna over the sauce bottles, but she didn't even look up. She was too busy cutting a doughnut in half and dunking the ends in her coffee before eating it, and she was bending her head right over her cup and making slurping noises to stop the coffee from running down her chin. I had to look the other way and try to keep my ears shut because it was awful.

Have you noticed what dreadful table manners grown-ups have, especially if they think nobody is watching? They dunk their bread in their soup and dip their biscuits in their tea and and wash mouthfuls of food down with swigs of wine and lick the butter off their knives and mash their mince and potatoes into a brown sludge on their plates, and I've even seen my dad pick up his cereal bowl and drink up the last of the milk when my mum wasn't looking. I wouldn't mind in the least, except that if we do anything like that we're told we're disgusting.

Anyway, Angela soon came back with two cokes, and a doughnut for me and a Kit-Kat for her. The doughnut was still warm and smelt delicious, and I was dying to eat it, but I noticed that a young woman had got stuck in the doorway with a pushchair and a load of shopping and three small kids so I thought I'd do my good deed for the day.

'Back in a sec,' I muttered to Angela, and I went to give a hand.

I wasn't gone much more than a minute, but when I got back to the table Evil Edna was just starting on a second doughnut. The greedy-guts! She's been and got herself another one, I thought. But then when I sat down I saw that my plate was empty. The glass of coke was still there but the doughnut had gone.

I stared at the empty plate, then looked under the table and all around the floor underneath. Finally I glared at Angela. She hadn't had time to eat a doughnut as well as most of her Kit-Kat, so she must have hidden it somewhere.

Angela had her mouth so full of Kit-Kat that she couldn't speak. Instead, she raised her eyebrows at me and jerked her thumb sideways at Evil Edna who, as calm as a coconut, was cutting that second doughnut in half.

I gave a little gasp of disbelief. Surely Evil Edna hadn't pinched my doughnut right off my plate while my back was turned. I looked helplessly at Angela and she nodded meaningfully at Evil Edna's bent head.

I drank my coke and watched as the first

half-doughnut was dunked and swallowed. Evil Edna must have felt me glowering at her because she suddenly looked up. And she had the nerve to give me one of her evil little smiles, the kind that make her eyes crinkle up and disappear into her face, like Farmer Lunnon's pig.

That did it. I wasn't going to sit there and let her grin at me while she ate *my* doughnut. I banged down my empty glass and scowled at Angela.

'Come on,' I said. 'I'm fed up with this.'

We both pushed our chairs back and got up, but as we turned to go I suddenly reached across the table, snatched the last bit of dough-nut from Evil Edna's plate, and stuffed it whole-sale into my mouth. Then we grabbed our trolleys and fled.

We ignored the scuffles and shouts from behind us and raced out between the sliding doors and into the sunshine. We hurtled down the concrete ramp towards the car park and Angela was hooting with laughter and yelling 'Good for you, Charlie!'. She must have been so excited that she forgot to look where she was going because her trolley suddenly lurched sideways into mine and I tripped and fell, losing my grip on the handle.

Angela skidded to a halt, only just saving her trolley from tipping over, but mine went on rumbling down the ramp all by itself.

'Ooh, sorry, Charlie!' she said, helping me to my feet. 'Are you OK?'

I glared at her and went racing after the runaway trolley as if my life depended on it, but the ramp was steep and smooth and the trolley thundered on getting faster and faster and I couldn't catch up.

'LOOK OUT!' I bellowed.

I was too late.

The trolley shot off the end of the ramp into the car park, just as a smart red Volvo was reversing out of its parking space.

CRASH!

The trolley collided with the back of the Volvo and they both stopped dead. Then the trolley slowly tipped over on its side, spilling my mum's shopping out all over the gravel.

Everything went quiet as people in the car park turned to stare. I stood gasping for breath with my face growing redder and redder as the door on the driver's side was flung open and a young man in a leather jacket and a black woolly hat leapt out of the car as though it was on fire. He glared at me furiously, hopping from one foot to the other in rage, while I stuffed my hands in my pockets and hunched my shoulders, expecting the biggest row in my life.

And then a very strange thing happened. An excited voice suddenly shrieked out from somewhere behind me, and a tall thin lady in a long green suit and a big yellow hat that made her look like a sunflower came running down the ramp.

'STOP HIM!' she shouted hysterically. 'THAT'S MY CAR!'

The young man cast one last venomous glance in my direction, then he turned and dashed off, weaving his way rapidly through the car park, jumping over the wall, and finally disappearing among the traffic on the main road.

All at once I found myself the hero of the day. Everybody crowded round to see if I was all right and to pat my shoulder and to say well done. There were plenty of willing hands to help me pick the shopping up and re-pack the trolley, and you won't believe it but there was no damage except for a couple of broken eggs. The supermarket manager sent for the police and I had to give a description of the car thief to a nice policewoman in a lovely uniform that made her look as smart as a carrot.

The sunflower lady was so delighted I'd prevented her car from being stolen that she insisted on giving me a reward, even though I told her the whole thing had been an accident.

'Accident or not,' she said, 'I'm still most grateful. My husband is always telling me I shouldn't leave the keys in the car. If it hadn't been for you that dreadful man would have got clean away with it.' And she stuffed a ten pound note in my anorak pocket in spite of my protests.

It was all so exciting that I completely forgot about Angela, but after a while people began to drift away and I had time to look round for her. And there she was, sitting on the wall, looking as mad as a mammoth because I was getting all the attention for once instead of her.

I grinned at her but she only scowled back. And when my mum drove in a few minutes later to pick us up with the shopping, Angela sat hunched in the back seat and didn't speak once all the way home, even though I chattered non-stop as I told my mum all about our adventure.

Angela had the last laugh though, as usual. After my mum and I had dropped her off and we were unpacking the bags of shopping in the kitchen and putting it all away, I put my hand on something soft and greasy stuffed in among the vegetables.

'Yuck!' I said, fishing it out and putting it on the worktop. Then my face went all hot as I realized what it was.

My mum stared. 'What on earth's that?' she said. 'It looks like a squashed doughnut.'

'It is a squashed doughnut,' I said, knowing there was only one way it could have got in the shopping. 'Angela bought it for me.'

It was a complicated story, and I didn't

bother to explain. But I knew it would be a long time before I dared go into the library and face Evil Edna again.

Chapter Five

My dad dipped his brush into emerald green watercolour paint and dabbed at his painting for a while. Then he leaned back in his chair to judge the effect.

'Have mermaid's knickers only got one leg-hole?' he asked my mum, as she came into the kitchen with her new red coat on, ready to go out. 'This doesn't look right somehow.'

I started to chuckle, but my mum scowled like a centipede with the gout and said, 'Really, Ted. You get worse. Mermaids don't wear knickers', which for some reason made my dad hoot with laughter and almost fall off his chair.

It was a Saturday, just after lunch. My dad and I had all my paints out on the kitchen table, and my mum was getting ready to go to a cookery demonstration with Auntie Sally. I was looking forward to having my dad all to myself for the afternoon, because he and I had decided to enter the Edgebourne Arts Society Painting Competition this year. And with my mum out of the way it would be a good opportunity to splosh about, without her complaining about us making a mess on the table or dribbling water on the floor.

'I'll just drape her tastefully in brown strands instead,' said my dad. And he winked at me as my mum went out and banged the door.

He mixed up some sludgy brown paint and we were both quiet for a while, absorbed in what we were doing. The clock ticked, the central heating boiler hummed, Daniel dozed in his basket, and it was all nice and peaceful. Then the door burst open and everything was spoiled.

'Hi, Charlie,' said Angela, marching in and taking off her anorak as if she owned the place. 'I've come to show you my new T-shirt. D'you think I look pretty?'

'Pretty horrible,' I told her sourly, although it wasn't true, because she looked fantastic, with her long hair brushed out loose over the shoulders of a soft cotton T-shirt the exact same shade of blue as her eyes.

'You shouldn't wear a T-shirt at lunchtime,' my dad told her. 'You should wear a lunch-shirt.'

Angela giggled and went to stand by his shoulder, looking down at his painting.

'Hi, Uncle Ted,' she said. 'Auntie Liz said I could come round. Can I do a painting as well?'

I gave a loud snort. 'Who, you?' I scoffed. 'You've said yourself you can't even draw the curtains.'

She put on a sulky face. 'Well, I won't get any better if I don't try,' she pointed out. 'And you know I've had a number of gold stars for art this term.'

I sniffed in disgust. The only gold star

Angela had was when Jane McLachlan helped her while Miss Sopwith wasn't looking.

'Come off it, Angela,' I said. 'You've only had one.'

'One *is* a number, isn't it?' said Angela, shaking her hair back with a smug smile, and my dad and I both had to laugh at that.

In the end she got her own way as usual. My dad gave her a clean sheet of paper, I lent her a pencil and my second-best brush, and she started doing a big splashy watercolour of a vase of flowers which really wasn't too bad if you looked at it with your eyes half shut.

My dad's painting wasn't bad either. It was an imaginary beach scene, with a sheltered little bay surrounded by trees. There were dolphins and seals playing in the water, birds flying in the sky and pecking about on the shore, and a smiling mermaid in a sort of seaweed bikini with shells in her hair sunning herself on a rock. It reminded you of dreams and holidays and fairy-tales and all kinds of lovely things.

As for me, I wasn't getting on well at all. Angela had spoilt my peaceful mood, and I had lost interest in my log cabin with snow-covered mountains and pine trees. My eyes kept straying to where Angela sat at the end of the table with a beam of sunshine lighting up her hair, and after a while I scrapped my painting and started another. And as soon as I'd started it I got that fizzy feeling in my stomach that tells you it's going to be good.

It was a head-and-shoulders portrait of Angela, with her blue eyes and her blue T-shirt and her golden hair glowing out from a dark background. I only used two colours, blue and gold, with just a touch of brown for the shadows, and although I worked quickly and had it finished in less than an hour, you really could tell who it was meant to be.

My dad glanced up after a while and noticed what I was doing.

'Wow!' he said, getting up and coming to look over my shoulder. 'That's terrific, Charlie. Don't do any more to it. You'll spoil the lovely fresh effect.'

Angela pushed her chair back and came to look too.

'Why, Charlie. It's me,' she beamed, dead

flattered that I'd painted a picture of her. 'It's brill. If it gets chosen for the exhibition I'll be hanging in the Community Centre and everybody will see me.'

'I'd rather see you hanging from the nearest tree,' I scowled, as I got up to wash the brushes in the sink, but I couldn't help feeling as pleased as anything all the same.

We each filled in one of the entry forms that my dad had picked up from the library. Then when the paintings were dry my dad wrapped each of them carefully in tissue paper to keep them clean, labelling Angela's and mine CHILDREN'S WATERCOLOUR SECTION – AGE GROUP 8 TO 10, and his ADULTS' WATERCOLOUR.

'Don't we have to put our names on them?' asked Angela.

My dad shook his head.

'Not until after the judging,' he told her. 'The entry forms have to be sent in separately. It's so the judges can't be accused of cheating or favouritism. The paintings are all given a number, and the judges have to choose the winners without knowing whose they are.'

'It's a good idea,' I said. I knew that Evil Edna was one of the judges and my painting wouldn't have a snowball's chance in hell if she saw my name on it. 'You have to go to the exhibition in April, and if your painting is one of the finalists it'll be hanging up and you get a label to stick on.'

'But that means anybody could claim my painting and say it was theirs,' objected Angela, and I sniggered rudely.

'Who'd be stupid enough to do that?' I said, and she gave me a look that was meant to shrivel me into a dead stick-insect on the spot.

My dad put the paintings on the hall table. 'Entries have to be in by Monday,' he said. 'I'll hand them in at the library on my way to work. And I'll pay our three pounds entry fee, since I don't suppose you girls have got any pocket money left, as usual.'

He grinned at us as we cleared the table and wiped the dribbles off it before my mum came home. 'They're giving cash prizes this year, I've heard,' he said. 'And do you know who's presenting them?'

Angela danced up and down in excitement.

'It's that fabulous Jason Dollarman from *West-enders*,' she said, going pink. 'That's really why I wanted to have a go.' She began to dance round the table, causing Daniel to wake up and leap out of his basket to growl and attack her trainers.

'Gerroff, you stupid spaniel,' she said, hopping on one foot and trying to push him away. Then she flung her arms round me in an impulsive hug. 'Ooh, Charlie, can you imagine winning first prize? Apart from getting some extra money for the holidays, you'd get a handshake from Jason Dollarman. Or maybe even a kiss!' And she pretended to swoon against the kitchen sink at the very thought.

We heard nothing for some weeks after that, and I was beginning to get impatient. Then one day the postman put two postcards in the door. One for Mr Ted Ellis and one for *Master* Charlie Ellis, both signed by Edna Eevle. She was pleased to inform us that the judging had now been completed, and that we were invited to attend the Edgebourne Arts Society Annual Exhibition on Saturday the nineteenth of April when the prize-giving was due to take place.

That meant there were only two more weeks to go, and I could hardly wait. I had a feeling in my bones that for once in my life I had managed to do something that was really a bit special.

On the morning of the exhibition I got up early. My mum and dad were still in bed, and I'm not allowed to disturb them on a Saturday, so I helped myself to a quick breakfast of yoghurt and banana. Then I went to the phone.

Angela answered in her special answering-the-phone voice.

'Edgebourne five-oh-five-oh-twooo?'

'Name this song and win a trip to Disney-land,' I said. 'You've got three guesses.' And I started to whistle a tune.

'Old Macdonald Had A Farm?' said Angela at once.

'Wrong,' I said. 'That's one.' And I whistled again.

'Knees Up Mother Brown?' said Angela.

'Wrong,' I said. 'That's two.' I whistled some more.

There was a silence.

Then, 'I know,' said Angela. 'It's Jesus Wants Me For A Sunbeam.'

'Wrong again,' I crowed jubilantly. 'It was The Day Granny's Hat Fell Down The Loo.'

Angela giggled. 'I bet your dad made that up,' she said, and I giggled too, because she was right.

'Did you ring up just for that?' she said, after we'd both had a good giggle.

'No,' I said. 'I wanted to remind you it's the art exhibition today. Shall we go together and get there early? The hall opens at nine, and I can't wait to see if my painting's been hung.'

'I can't wait to get a kiss from Jason Dollarman,' said Angela. 'But I'm off to Barlow now with my mum. She's buying me a new sweater specially for the occasion. Let's go to the exhibition together after lunch, Charlie. OK?' And she put the phone down without waiting for my reply.

My mum and dad got up at last, but they didn't want to go early either. My mum had to get her hair done, although why she had to choose that day I'll never know. And even my dad had something else he wanted to do first.

95

'Sorry, bonny lass,' he said. 'I've got a tricky letter to write to the bank manager, and I really want to get it into the post this morning. I was planning on going to the exhibition this afternoon. The prize-giving's not till three anyway.'

I never understand why it is that whenever *you* want to do something, *they* always want to do something else. And why is what *they* want to do always more important? It doesn't seem fair.

In the end I went by myself.

'We'll see you there about twelve,' said my mum, dropping me off at the corner of the High Street near the Community Centre. 'We'll have lunch at MacDougal's afterwards if you want.'

I scowled and stomped off with my head in the air. They didn't seem to care whether my painting had won a prize or not, and it would take more than a rotten beefburger and a few lousy chips before I forgave them for that.

I went into the exhibition hall, where a crowd was already beginning to gather. Inside, the walls were covered from floor to ceiling with paintings of all shapes and sizes. They had all been numbered and divided into sections, and some of them had coloured rosettes and cards pinned on them saying things like ADULTS' WATERCOLOUR – THIRD PRIZE and CHILDREN'S OILS, AGE GROUP 13 to 15 – FIRST PRIZE. There was no sign of my dad's painting, nor of mine, and I was looking round a bit aimlessly when I suddenly spotted Angela.

You can imagine my astonishment. She was in the little queue that was forming at the judges' desk at the back of the hall, under a big white banner which said, EXHIBITORS – COLLECT YOUR STICKY LABELS HERE, and she went all pink and embarrassed when she saw me.

'Charlie!' she said. 'I didn't think you were coming till this afternoon.'

'Well, I could say the same about you,' I retorted. 'You said you were going to buy a sweater. And what are you doing in this queue? Is your painting in the exhibition?'

She went pinker still and waved her hand vaguely towards the other end of the hall.

'Yes, it's down there,' she said. 'In the Children's Watercolour Section.' So I left her in the queue and went to look.

My dad had explained what it was you had to do. You had to look round the exhibition, and if you found your painting hanging up you had to show your postcard from Evil Edna to one of the judges at the desk. This proved that you'd entered the competition and paid your entry fee. In return they gave you a peel-off sticky label on which you had to write your name and the title of your painting. Then you could label your picture so that everybody could see who the prizewinners were. It was a bit complicated, but it worked. At least it had always worked until today. Until Mitch the Witch messed up the system, that is.

I had to push my way into the Children's Watercolour Section, because a crowd had gathered to ooh and aah over the winning painting, which was on a special table all by itself.

At first I couldn't see the painting at all. Then I managed to squeeze past a large lady with bunches of plastic shopping bags hanging from her wrists like giant fruit dangling on a tree. And my heart began to thump like a steam-hammer under my pink Damart thermal vest.

Pinned to a board standing on the table, with a big red rosette on one corner and a card which said NUMBER 43, AGE GROUP 8 to 10 – FIRST PRIZE propped up in front, was a portrait painted in blue and gold. A head-and-shoulders portrait of someone with blue eyes and a blue T-shirt and long golden hair gleaming in a patch of sunshine.

My portrait of Angela.

It had won first prize.

'Are you all right?' a lady with purple hair and lipstick to match asked me, because I gave a sort of yelp as if I had been struck by lightning.

'Yes, thanks,' I gulped. 'I'm just a bit gobsmacked, that's all. That's my painting.'

'Coo,' said the lady. 'You are clever. Mine didn't even get hung. You'd better go and claim your sticker at the desk.'

I felt so excited it was like having bubbles bursting in my brain, but I pulled myself together and hurried back to the desk. On my way there I bumped into Angela, hurrying in the opposite direction with a white sticky label in her hand. I grabbed her arm.

'Angela, I've won!' I burst out. 'My painting's won first prize!'

She shook my hand off her sleeve and stared at me. Her eyes were green instead of blue, and that's always a bad sign.

'Don't be silly, Charlie,' she said. 'You can't have done. There's only one first prize for our age group, and it's mine.'

I knew there was some mistake, because I hadn't even seen her vase of flowers hanging up, but I didn't have time to argue. So I left her there and joined the queue at the desk, and after a long wait I got to the front at last.

I avoided Evil Edna who was standing there with a face like a smacked backside, and showed my postcard to a young man with haystack hair and shredded wheat eyebrows who gave me a sticky label and a black felt-tip pen in exchange.

I rested the label on a corner of the desk and printed in my neatest writing POR-

TRAIT OF ANGELA by CHARLIE ELLIS. I gave the pen back to the haystack man and told him the number of my picture so he could tick it off his list. Then I scooted back through the crowd.

There was an even bigger swarm round the table by now, and I had to really shove to get near it. Then my heart slowly turned over and slithered down my legs to my knees.

The painting had a sticker on already.

SELF-PORTRAIT, it said, by ANGELA MITCHELL.

And there she was, smirking all over her face, while people patted her on the shoulder and said, 'Coo, how clever,' and, 'Isn't she brilliant,' and stuff like that.

I gasped a couple of times because the air had somehow been pumped out of my lungs. Then I took a deep breath, stuck my chin out and stood as tall as I could, for I had made up my mind that she wasn't going to get away with it.

'THAT'S NOT HER PAINTING,' I announced firmly in a loud voice. 'IT'S MINE!' And I stepped forward, peeled her rotten sticker off, and stuck mine on in its place.

Everybody stopped talking and turned to stare at me, like they did at my cousin Fiona's wedding reception when I dropped my sausage-on-a-stick into the big glass bowl of fruit punch and accidentally said a very rude word.

Angela snatched up her sticker from the floor where I'd flung it, peeled mine off, and stuck hers back on again. My sticker was still in her hand, so I grabbed it from her and stuck it back on over hers. Then I announced again, even louder this time.

'THIS ISN'T HER PAINTING. IT'S MINE!'

Angela hissed like a tiger with the toothache. Then she peeled my label off again, screwed it up into a tiny ball and flicked it away over the heads of the crowd.

Suddenly the spell broke and they all starting talking at once, with Angela saying, 'Charlie Ellis, how dare you!' and everybody else saying, 'Ooh, fancy! They're both claiming the same painting!' and the lady with the purple lipstick saying, 'They couldn't both have painted it,' and me getting red in the face with determination and Angela getting even redder with sheer rage. Then a voice said, 'Excuse me, what's going on here?' and old haystack-hair himself came pushing through the mob.

He looked at me, he looked at Angela, then he frowned at the list in his hand. 'I seem to have two ticks for painting number forty-three,' he said. 'Whose is this painting, please?'

'It's mine,' I said promptly.

'It's mine,' said Angela, giving me a swift kick on the shin.

The man looked at the Angela's label. 'Self-portrait by Angela Mitchell,' he read aloud. Then he looked again from me to Angela and back.

'It can't be yours,' he said to me. 'It doesn't even look like you. If it's a self-portrait, it must be hers. It's the spitting image of her.'

'But that doesn't prove she painted it!' I cried, blinking back tears of frustration. How could anybody be so stupid!

I could see he didn't believe me, and my heart turned over again and slithered from my knees to my feet. What on earth could I do to convince him? Only my dad could vouch for me, and he wasn't here. Parents never seem to be there when you really need them, have you noticed? And if you don't want them around it's impossible to get rid of them. It's very strange.

Anyway just then I heard a familiar voice behind me, and if my heart hadn't been in my shoes already it would have sunk even lower, because it was Miss Collingwood, our headmistress, who was also one of the judges, and who thinks the sun shines out of Angela's bottom.

'What's all the commotion about, Dennis?' she said, and the crowd fell back to let her through. 'Is there a dispute about ownership? It's never happened before.'

I stared glumly at the floor while Haystack Dennis explained the situation. Miss Collingwood listened without saying a word until she'd heard the whole story. Then she stepped forward and unpinned the painting from its board.

'There's only one way to settle this,' she said, giving Angela and me both a sharp look. 'We'll tear it in two, and they can have half each.' And she held the painting in the middle at the top, ready to tear.

There was another long silence while everybody waited to see what we would do. Then Angela gave me a spiteful little smile and tossed her head.

'All right,' she said. 'Tear it in two. I don't care!'

'No, wait!' I said hastily. 'Don't tear it. It'll be ruined!'

It was probably stupid of me, but that painting was the best thing I'd ever done in my life, and I couldn't bear the thought of it being spoilt. Not even if it meant that Angela won the competition instead of me. In any case, she would know as well as I did who'd really won.

'Let Angela have it,' I blurted out. 'If she's that desperate to win the prize.'

And an amazing thing happened. Miss Collingwood pinned the painting back on its board. Then she gave me a huge, beaming smile and put her arm round my shoulders.

'Come with me and get a new sticker, Charlie,' she said. 'The picture must be yours, as Angela doesn't seem to care whether it's torn in half or not. She obviously doesn't read her Bible.'

She turned to Angela with a severe look. 'I'll see you in my study first thing on Monday morning, young lady,' she said. 'And in the meantime I advise you to read in your Bible about the Judgement of Solomon.'

Well, of course Angela was boiling with rage, but there wasn't a thing she could do about it. She gave me a murderous look and went flouncing off, red-faced and furious.

I didn't care two hoots. Miss Collingwood took me back to the desk and I wrote out a new label to stick on the painting. And when my mum and dad came to get me at twelve, they were just as pleased and proud as I was, even though my dad's painting hadn't been hung, and off we went to celebrate at MacDougal's with chips and coke and the biggest burgers on the menu.

But that wasn't the best bit.

It wasn't even the best bit when we went back at three o'clock for the prizegiving, and Jason Dollarman called my name out and gave me an envelope with fifty pounds in it and everybody clapped and cheered.

And it wasn't even the best bit when he

said, 'Well done, Charlie!' and gave me a kiss on the cheek in front of all those people, making me blush from the top of my head to the tips of my toes.

It was when a sudden commotion started at the back of the hall, and Angela, in her new yellow fluffy sweater that made her look like an Easter chick, had to be helped outside by her mother because she had suddenly started shouting and crying and throwing herself about in some sort of hysterical attack.

It might be horrible of me, but that was really the best bit of all.

Chapter Six

My dad is my favourite person in the world, so when he started acting in that peculiar way it seemed like the worst calamity of all. And of course it was Angela who told me he was up to something.

She dropped the first bombshell on a bright breezy Tuesday in March when we were sitting in the playground with some of the other girls, chatting about the coming Easter holidays and watching the boys playing football with somebody's filthy old trainer.

'Laurence Parker's going to Spain for Easter,' said Jane McLachlan. 'Lucky beggar.' She leaned back against the wall and giggled. 'I'm going to stay with my Grandma in Scotland again. She lives on a farm and when you go for a walk you get cowpat all over your wellies.'

'Well, at least you're going *some*where,' said Angela. 'I'm going nowhere at all, and neither's Charlie. My dad's been made repugnant, and Charlie's dad's always hard up anyway.'

For once I didn't laugh at her mistake. Nobody's allowed to say things like that about my dad.

'No, he isn't,' I said indignantly. 'That's not true.'

It was true we weren't having an Easter holiday this year, but it wasn't because my dad was hard up. It was because he was too busy at the office and couldn't get away. At least that's what my mum had told me.

'Well, he's always complaining he's hard up,' retorted Angela. 'Maybe that's why he keeps creeping off in disguise. Maybe he's trying to make money by selling secrets to the Russians.' She lowered her voice to a dramatic whisper. 'Maybe he's a *spy*!'

Most of the girls laughed at that because they're used to Angela and her jokes, but that awful Delilah Jones turned and stared at me as if my chin had sprouted red and white spotted toadstools.

'Don't be silly, Angela,' I said. 'My dad only works in the council office. He couldn't possibly be a spy. And what do you mean, creeping off in disguise? What are you talking about?'

She couldn't say anything more just then because the bell rang and we had to go inside. It was English that afternoon, my favourite subject, but for the life of me I couldn't concentrate. We had to write an essay about what we would do if we had three wishes. All I could think of was that my first wish would be for a big wooden crate, my second would be for two thousand fat black spiders, the hairy-legged scuttling sort that Angela is terrified of, and my third would be for Angela to be sealed up in the crate with the spiders and put on board the next spaceship to the moon. I didn't think Miss Sopwith would like that very much so I ended up not writing anything at all which was worse.

'You'd better do your essay at home this evening, Charlie,' said Miss Sopwith crossly when she collected the papers at half-past three. 'Perhaps that will teach you not to doodle and gaze out of the window half the afternoon.'

Angela caught up with me as I went stomping out of the school gate.

'I'm sorry, Charlie,' she said putting her arm around me. 'But if your dad is thinking of reflecting to the Russians it's better you should know, isn't it?'

'You mean *defect*ing,' I said scornfully. 'And anyway, it's all lies. My dad could never be a spy.'

Angela shrugged. 'All right,' she said. 'So why does he keep sneaking off with that woman?'

I stopped dead in the middle of the pavement and stared at her. Then I hooted with laughter, because this time she'd gone too far. I may be a mug but I'm not an entire tea-set.

'My dad? Sneaking off with a woman?' I snorted. Then I leaned forward and prodded her in the chest. 'And what woman's that, Miss Cleverclogs Mitchell?'

Angela lost her temper at that. She put her face close to mine and spoke slowly and distinctly as if I was a ninety-six-year-old Martian peasant.

'The *blonde* who *picks him up* in a *red car*, Miss Cleverbloomers Ellis!' she said. 'On *Tuesday* evenings. When he's *supposed* to be playing *badminton* at the Community Centre with *my dad*!' Then she turned and flounced off, leaving me standing on the pavement as if my feet had turned to concrete.

I stared after her for a minute, then I gave myself a shake and set off home. It couldn't be true, but I still got a funny feeling when I thought about what she'd said. For the last few weeks my dad *had* played badminton every Tuesday with Uncle Jim, which seemed a bit odd because my dad has always been a tennis man and hates badminton. He always says if it was a half-decent game it would be called goodminton.

My mum was on the phone in the hall when I went in the back door.

'Yes, Sally, we've finally made up our minds,' she was saying. 'What? Oh yes, you're right, I'll have to start learning the language.' She gave a little laugh at that, then, 'No, we haven't told Charlie yet. So don't say anything to Angela, will you? You know what kids are like . . .'

She must have heard me in the kitchen because her voice suddenly trailed off.

'I'll see you later, Sally,' she said hurriedly. 'Charlie's just come in. 'Bye.'

She came into the kitchen.

'Hello, poppet,' she said. 'You look pale. Are you all right?'

'Haven't told Charlie what?' I said.

'Oh, nothing,' said my mum vaguely, looking out of the window and not at me. 'Let's take Daniel for a walk, shall we, Charlie? It's a lovely afternoon.'

'No thanks,' I said. 'I've got an essay to write.'

And I rushed upstairs and flung myself on my bed.

I lay there for more than an hour just staring at the ceiling. There was something going on I wasn't supposed to know about, and whatever it was, my mum was in on it too. What on earth was all that about learning the language? Maybe my dad's job was more important than I thought. Maybe he *was* a spy. Maybe he really was going to defect, and we'd all have to go and live in Russia. What would happen to Daniel if we did that? By the time I heard my dad's car come scrunching into the drive I had worried myself into a right old state. I hurled myself down the stairs and into his arms as soon as he opened the front door.

'Hey, give over, bonny lass,' he laughed, untangling my arms from around his neck. 'Are you trying to strangle your poor old dad? Who's going to polish your cornflakes and pour milk on your shoes every morning if you do that?'

I felt better at once. He gave my mum a hug and everything seemed normal. Angela had made the whole thing up, I decided. The next time I saw her I'd give her a kick up the backside.

My dad put the dishes in the sink after dinner.

'I'll wash up, Liz,' he said. 'But I won't bother with coffee. I'm calling for Jim at seven.'

My mum put a spoonful of coffee into her Garfield mug.

'Have you got clean sports kit, Ted?' she asked. 'I don't remember seeing any shorts in the wash this week. Or for the last few weeks either, come to that.'

'Oh, they're not very dirty,' said my dad airily. 'They'll be OK.'

My mum banged the mug down on the work-top.

'Ted!' she said crossly. 'Don't tell me your sweaty things have been in that bag all these weeks without being washed. They'll be all crumpled up and stinking. What will people think!'

She went into the hall and pulled my dad's sports bag out from under the stairs.

'I'll give them a quick wash now,' she said. 'They'll dry in less than half an hour in the tumble drier.'

'No, leave them, Liz. There isn't time,' said my dad hastily.

He left the sink with soapy water dripping from his wrists and tried to stop her, but he was too late. My mum had already tipped the badminton kit out onto the table.

A white sports shirt. White shorts. A pair of white socks. The lovely blue and green stripy towel that my mum won't have in the bathroom because it clashes with the pink bathroom suite. And they were all clean and neatly folded, with smart creases in the shorts as if they'd come straight from the ironing board.

My mum stared. 'This stuff's still clean,' she said. She held the folded towel against her cheek. 'The towel's not even damp. Didn't you have a shower after the game?'

I looked at my dad. His face had gone a bit red, and for a moment he couldn't think of anything to say. Then he laughed.

'I've just remembered,' he said. 'I chucked everything in the washing machine myself. On Saturday. While you and Charlie were shopping in Barlow.' He stuffed the sports things hurriedly back in the bag. 'You're always telling me I should learn how to drive the washing machine,' he said. 'Well, I have.'

My mum looked at him in astonishment. Then she went back to making her coffee. 'Not before time,' she said tartly. 'Pity you didn't throw a few sheets in while you were at it.'

I could see my dad breathing a sigh of relief because my mum had swallowed his story. And I breathed one too, for his sake. But I didn't believe a word of it. Not if what Angela had told me was true. But why was my dad lying to my mum? My brain buzzed with questions.

'Can I go round and see Angela?' I said. 'She might go with me to take Daniel for a walk.'

'Yes, all right,' said my mum. 'I'll be popping round to Sally's myself later on.' She ruffled my hair fondly. 'Get well wrapped up, poppet. That March breeze is a bit chilly.'

I put on my thick quilted jacket that makes me look short and fat like an overweight Eskimo and my woolly pompon hat that my gran knitted for my birthday. Daniel was already jumping up and down at the back door, so off we went down the drive and round the corner to Angela's house.

Angela opened the door, and as soon as she saw me she grabbed both my hands and pulled me inside. I let her take me upstairs to her playroom over the garage, and I sat on a bean bag on the floor with Daniel's head in my lap.

'I don't believe any of your rubbish about that woman,' I told her sternly. 'But if you know anything about where my dad goes on Tuesday evenings you'd better tell me. I know for a fact he doesn't play badminton.'

I expected her to say I told you so but she sat on the bean bag beside me, all sympathy.

'I was in the park last Tuesday with my cousin Dominic,' she explained. '*And* the Tuesday before. And both times I saw your dad. He was picked up by that blonde woman I told you about, in the red car. He didn't see me, and I haven't told anybody else, honest, Charlie. Not even my mum.' She narrowed her eyes and made her face go all crafty. 'I wanted to be Shylock Holmes, and do some more detective work. I wanted to make sure he really is a spy first.'

I gave her a Paddington hard stare, wondering whether she was telling the truth this time.

'You don't have to believe me, Charlie,' she said. 'We'll follow him, and see where he goes.'

I scowled at her in disgust. 'Go snooping after my own dad?' I said, pushing her off the bean bag. 'That's awful.'

'It's the only way to convince you he's up to something,' she said, rubbing her elbow where she'd banged it on the floor.

I put my chin in my hands and thought about it for a while.

'All right,' I muttered at last. 'We'll follow him. I don't like it one bit, but I've got to know.'

Angela began pulling things out of the chest of drawers where she keeps her dressing-up clothes.

'Put these on, Charlie,' she said. She handed me a long velvet skirt which must have been her grandmother's, an imitation fur cape with ermine tails, and a huge straw hat trimmed with roses, the sort that people wear to go to garden parties with the Queen.

'What's this?' I said blankly, and her eyes danced.

'Disguise, stupid,' she said. 'You don't want your dad to recognize you, do you?'

'No, I don't,' I said, and started putting the things on. I pulled the long skirt over my jeans, draped the cape around my shoulders, and plonked the straw bonnet on my head, stuffing my knitted woolly hat into my pocket out of the way. When I was ready I turned to look at Angela.

She was wearing tight leggings in pink and lime green, a pair of suede boots several sizes too big for her, and a bomber jacket with sleeves that hung over her wrists. She had tucked all her hair up into a baseball cap with a plastic eyeshade, and a false beard and moustache covered half her face. She looked like something out of the Muppet Show.

Daniel thought it was brilliant fun, and kept growling and tugging at the hem of my skirt with his teeth.

'You look fabulous, Charlie,' giggled Angela through the beard. 'But we must do something with Daniel. We don't want your dad to recognize him either.' She delved back into the drawer and pulled out a tartan scarf, which she fastened round Daniel's middle like a corset. Then she put a baby's frilly bonnet on his head, and tied the ribbon in a bow under his chin. And I couldn't help laughing then, in spite of feeling as if the bottom had fallen out of my sailing boat in a rough sea infested with sharks.

Daniel capered excitedly about, enjoying every minute, but there wasn't time to play games, for just then we heard the doorbell ring and my dad's voice in the hall.

There was a short silence, then we heard footsteps in the drive. Angela peeped out of the window from behind the curtain.

'There they go, Charlie,' she said. 'Are you ready?'

Off we went down the stairs and along the street, and it was just like being in one of those spy films on the telly. We kept our two dads in sight as they strolled along together with their sports bags and badminton rackets, and we followed not too closely behind, dodging into people's driveways or behind parked cars if either of them seemed about to turn round. We got some funny looks from passers-by, I

can tell you, but luckily we didn't meet anybody we knew.

They reached the T-junction at the end of
Russell Road and stopped. Angela and I dived
behind the telephone box to watch.

My dad said something to Uncle Jim. Then
they parted and walked off in opposite direc-
tions. Uncle Jim went left towards the Community Centre, and my dad turned right towards
the park. My legs felt like candy-floss and
Angela had to almost drag me along the road
and round the corner.

'Come on, Charlie!' she urged. 'We'll lose
him if we don't get a move on.'

The park came into view and my dad
crossed the main road to the gates. Angela
pushed me behind a fence on some waste
ground on the opposite side. We crouched
down and peered through the gaps in the
fence.

After a quick look up and down the road
my dad took a blue cotton sun-hat out of his
pocket and put it on, pulling the brim well
down over his face. Then he took a pair of
sunglasses from another pocket and put them

on as well, even though the sun was already setting and the evening had turned cloudy.

I watched, almost forgetting to breathe, while my dad paced back and forth, glancing now and again at his watch. Then a red car, driven by a young woman with blonde hair and huge gold earrings, pulled close to the kerb and stopped.

My dad took another quick glance up and down the road. Then he got into the car and they drove away.

'There! What did I tell you? Shylock Holmes was right!' said Angela triumphantly.

The next morning was even worse. After a rotten night, tossing and turning and worrying and fretting, I got up feeling as limp as an old lettuce. On my way down the stairs I noticed a brown envelope lying on the doormat in the hall.

I picked it up. It had a Barlow postmark and was addressed to Mr and Mrs Ellis, and my knees went wobbly when I saw the address of the sender on the back.

Jenkinson and Partners, Solicitors and Estate Agents, Thames Walk, Barlow.

Oh crumbs, I thought. A letter from my

dad's solicitors. Maybe my dad was selling our house. Maybe we really were going to live in Siberia or Outer Mongolia. Oh double crumbs.

My dad was sitting at the kitchen table dressed for the office and eating half a grapefruit. He reached for the cornflakes packet when he saw me coming into the kitchen.

'Here she comes,' he announced. 'Her name may be Marge, but there's no point in buttering her up.'

He laughed like a drain and poured a heap of cornflakes into my Peter Rabbit cereal bowl that I've had since I was two.

I didn't even smile. I sat down in my place and put the letter from the solicitor in front of him on the table.

'What's that?' said my mum, coming into the kitchen in her dressing-gown. 'Is it from Mr Howe? It must be about the . . .'

'I'll open it later,' said my dad quickly, giving her a warning look. He handed me the milk jug and grinned.

'Wake up, Charlie. You look half dead this morning,' he said.

'She was like that last night as well,' said my

mum, spooning tea-leaves into the teapot. 'I couldn't get a word out of her at Sally's. See if you can cheer her up.'

'Right. What do you get if you cross a greedy cat with a roast duck?' said my dad at once, and I gazed down into my cornflakes and heaved a sigh.

'A duck-filled fatty-puss,' I said gloomily. 'You asked me that yesterday, Dad. And the day before.'

My dad burst out laughing, as if it was the funniest thing I'd ever said.

'Talking about ducks,' he chuckled. 'I've heard Donald Duck isn't all he's quacked up to be.'

I got up from the table then because I couldn't stand any more of it.

'I don't want any breakfast, Mum,' I said. 'I think I'll get ready for school.'

My mum felt my forehead. 'Aren't you feeling well, poppet?' she asked. 'I hope it's not 'flu. Maybe you should have the day off.'

I pulled myself away. 'I'm fine, Mum,' I insisted. 'I just need some fresh air. It's games this morning, so I'll be better off at school.'

'Get well wrapped up, then, sweetheart,' said my dad, and I ran out of the kitchen and slammed the door.

I was halfway up the stairs when the phone rang in the hall. I ran down again and picked it up.

A man's voice asked for Mr Ellis.

'I'll get him,' I said. Then I said politely, 'Who is it please?' because my mum says you should always ask who it is before calling someone to the phone.

'It's David Howe, of Jenkinson and Partners,' the voice said, and I dropped the receiver on the table because it had suddenly turned red-hot in my hand.

I took a deep breath and put my head round the kitchen door.

'It's for you, Dad,' I told him. 'It's Mr Howe.' My dad grabbed the envelope off the table and came to the phone, muttering, 'How now, Mr Howe,' to himself on the way.

I ran upstairs to my room, but I left the door open so I could hear what he said. I know you shouldn't eavesdrop, but there are times when there's a good excuse, and this was one of them.

'How now . . . er . . . hello, Mr Howe,' said my dad. 'Yes, thanks. It came this morning. No, I haven't opened it yet.'

A short pause, then, 'Yes, the sooner the better. This afternoon? Yes, I can leave work early. We'll come into your office at about half-past two? Thanks. 'Bye.' He went back into the kitchen and shut the door.

I sorted my things out for school and stuffed my games kit into my satchel any old how. Then I got myself into a flap because I could only find one trainer even though I hunted high and low for the other. I frowned at Daniel who was still fast asleep on the end of my bed.

'If you've buried it in the rhubarb patch again you're in for it,' I told him crossly. 'Those trainers were brand new and cost the best part of thirty pounds.'

I hoped I'd find it in the changing room at school, because there was no more time to look for it just then. My mum was calling up the stairs.

'Charlie? Are you ready? Angela's here for you.'

So there was nothing else for it except to

trudge off to school, and I was in trouble as soon as I arrived because of course I'd forgotten all about my essay. Old Soppy made me stay in the classroom and do it while everybody else went out onto the school field to play rounders.

The essay didn't take me long to write, because I knew what my three wishes were now, but even so I didn't get to play games because my trainer wasn't in the changing room where I thought I might have left it, and old Soppy wouldn't let me play in my ordinary shoes.

It wasn't until play-time and the boys were playing football as usual that it occurred to me to have a closer look at that old trainer they'd been kicking around for a week in the dust. I waited until one of the boys kicked it in my direction, then I ran forward and picked it up.

It was filthy and covered in mud but I could still just make out the name written on the inside with black felt pen. It was my mum's writing and it said Charlie Ellis. And it wasn't one of my old ones because they'd been from Marks and Spencers and the maker's name on this one was Strike.

I stared at it in disbelief. Then Laurence Parker came and tried to snatch it out of my hand.

'Aw, come on, Charlie. Let's have it back,' he said. 'Angela said you didn't need it any more.'

I was so stunned I let him take it. I looked round for Angela, but she was giggling in a corner with a gang of girls and I knew they were all talking about me. So I marched off with my head in the air and ignored her for the rest of the day.

I ran all the way home at half-past three and when I got there my dad's car was in the drive. I let myself into the kitchen, and found my mum and dad sitting at the table. My dad was looking through a pile of papers and my mum was pouring tea.

'Hello, Charlie,' she said. 'You're just in time for a cup of tea. I thought we'd try something different for a change. It's Lapsang Souchong.'

She poured another cup and I sat down. I sipped the hot tea, and it was nice. It had a strange smokey flavour, but nice. And somehow comforting.

While I sipped I stole a furtive peep sideways at the papers on the table. The top one was an official-looking document, with a red seal and what seemed like a legal sort of stamp. I could see my mum's signature, and my dad's, and the names of two witnesses.

My dad took a swig of tea and spluttered.

'Good grief, Liz,' he snorted. 'D'you call that tea? It's like drinking kippers!'

He poured his cupful down the sink and made a fresh cup with an ordinary teabag. Then he sat down again.

I looked from one to the other but I couldn't guess anything from their faces. There was silence for a minute, then my dad glanced at my mum.

'We'll tell her now, shall we?' he said. 'Now that all this stuff's been signed and everything.'

'Yes, Ted, I think we should,' said my mum. 'Do you want to tell her or shall I?'

'I will, if you like,' said my dad.

My heart skipped a beat and almost stopped altogether. I had a sudden feeling that nothing would ever be the same again. I banged my cup down in its saucer and jumped up in such a panic that I knocked my chair to the floor.

'DON'T TELL ME!' I shouted, putting my hands over my ears. 'I DON'T WANT TO KNOW!'

Then I fled upstairs to my room and howled my eyes out on the bed.

I had to stop after a while, partly because Daniel was jumping up and down on top of me, but mainly because the phone had started ringing in the hall and I wanted to hear what was said.

'Who?' queried my dad. 'Miss Sopwith? Oh, Charlie's teacher!' He laughed and said, 'What has she been up to now?' as if I was the naughtiest girl in the school. There was a pause while he listened, and when he spoke again his voice had gone all serious.

'No, certainly not, Miss Sopwith. I can't think why. Yes, of course I'll have a word with her. Thank you for letting me know.'

I was sitting up on the bed, drying my eyes on my Snoopy pyjamas and trying to stop hiccupping, when my dad came into the room. He sat beside me and put his arm round me.

'Miss Sopwith is very upset about your essay, Charlie,' he said. 'She tells me that if you had three wishes you'd wish the same wish three times.'

I sniffed dismally. 'I wanted to make sure it would come true,' I gulped, and my dad gave me his hanky to blow my nose on. That was a great comfort, too, because hankies are like toothbrushes. You only share them with the people you love.

'But why would you wish your dad to be honest and truthful and always stay out of trouble?' he said. 'It's a waste of good wishes, if you ask me. That's what I intend to do anyway. At least I'll have a darned good try.'

I digested this for a minute.

'So you're not selling secrets or spying for the Russians or planning to run away to Moscow?' I said, the words tumbling out all in a rush.

Then I jumped off the bed and flung my arms around his neck because he was falling about laughing as if it was the most ridiculous thing he'd ever heard in his life.

'Don't talk daft, Charlie!' he spluttered, rolling about on the bed. 'Whatever gave you that idea?'

Daniel leaped on top of him and they rolled about together, while I danced round my bedroom as if Prince Charming had invited me to the ball.

'Right, Charlie,' said my dad, when we'd all calmed down a bit. 'I want to know what all this is about.'

So we sat down again on the bed and out it came. About him not playing badminton on Tuesdays. About Angela and me seeing him with the woman in the red car. About me hearing my mum on the phone to Auntie Sally and about my mum having to start learning the language. About him getting the letter from the solicitor and going to sign papers at the solicitor's office with my mum. And about me putting two and two together.

'And making seven hundred and sixty-three,' said my dad ruefully when I'd finished. 'You've got the wrong end of the stick entirely, you mutt.'

And then he started to explain. It took quite a long time, and my mum was shouting up the stairs that our supper was ready by the time he came to the end. But at last I knew what was going on, and the bottom had been put back into my world.

The truth was that my mum and dad had bought a cottage. A little holiday cottage by the sea in Northumberland, near my gran, where we could go for holidays without us all having to squash into my gran's tiny house, and where we could take Daniel without the hassle of having to find somewhere that allowed dogs. The letters and legal papers and phone calls and visits to the solicitor had all been about that. And the only language my mum was going to have to learn was the Tyneside dialect.

'It's a great little place, Charlie,' said my dad. 'Right by a lovely sandy bay. I'll show you some photos after supper.' He grinned at me and ruffled my hair. 'We didn't want you to know anything until it was all settled. In case the deal fell through and you were disappointed.'

He got up and stretched his arms. 'And that's why we didn't book an Easter holiday this year, bonny lass,' he said. 'We'll be driving up to the cottage as soon as school breaks up next week.'

I was so excited I wanted to pack my bags there and then. But there were still a couple of things I didn't understand.

'What about Tuesday evenings?' I said. 'The funny hat and dark glasses? And who's the lady in the red car?'

My dad grinned. 'That's Mrs Randell,' he said. 'She's a private driving instructor, the one who taught your mum. She's an absolute genius behind the wheel.'

He got up, opened the bedroom door and peered out. Then he closed it again, his finger to his lips.

'Your mum doesn't know yet, but I've been having advanced driving lessons,' he said. 'Every Tuesday evening, when I'm supposed to be playing badminton.'

He chuckled and did a little jig on my bedside rug. 'Jim agreed to the badminton alibi because I don't want to tell your mum yet. Not until after I've taken my test next week. She'd laugh her socks off if I failed. You won't tell her anything, will you Charlie?'

My mum yelled up the stairs that if we liked cold spaghetti bolognese it was all the same to her.

'I won't tell her,' I said.

Then we went downstairs for supper, and I scoffed the biggest plate of spaghetti you ever saw in your life, with a mountain of grated cheese.

I managed to say nothing to Angela about any of it for a whole week, even though she was still keen on solving the mystery, and kept pestering me to tell her if I'd found out anything more. Then on the Tuesday evening, while my dad was out taking his test, I invited her round for a game of Monopoly, which I hate playing with her because she sneaks hotels onto her property when I'm not looking and then swears they've been there all the time.

Anyway, Angela and my mum and I were sitting round the kitchen table at about half-past eight when all at once the back door burst open and in pranced my dad. He had a huge bunch of flowers in one hand and a huge box of chocolates in the other and an even huger grin on his face.

'Ted! Have you been to the pub?' said my mum, tutting crossly. Then she stopped and gaped open-mouthed as a young woman with piled-up blonde hair and long dangling earrings followed my dad into the kitchen.

'Jenny Randell!' exclaimed my mum.

'Hello, Liz,' said Mrs Randell, smiling. 'Nice to see you again. How are you?'

'Charlie, I passed!' shouted my dad, shoving the flowers and chocolates at my astonished mum. I flung my arms round him and danced him round the table and in no time at all it was like Paddy's Market with me and my dad shouting and laughing and Daniel bouncing and barking and my mum bellowing at us above the din and Angela gaping at us each in turn and wondering what the heck was going on.

Well, eventually we all calmed down. My dad explained about the driving test, and the lessons on Tuesday evenings, and my mum was thrilled to bits that he'd passed.

'Congratulations, darling!' she beamed. 'I knew you'd do it one of these days. But I wish you'd told me. I might have been able to give you a few tips.'

My dad winked at me as she pinned his certificate proudly on the wall. Then he put the kettle on for coffee and we all sat round the table laughing and chatting like old friends.

At first Angela didn't know whether to be glad or sorry. Of course she was pleased to learn that my dad wasn't a spy after all, but she wasn't really pleased that all her detective work had been for nothing. And she certainly wasn't pleased when it came out that I'd known for a whole week without telling her. She sat there scowling for a while with nobody taking the slightest bit of notice of her, then without saying goodbye or goodnight or kiss my elbow or anything, she got up and walked out.

She was even less pleased the next day, the last day of term. We were sitting in the playground as usual, and this time it was me who raised the topic of holidays.

'Does your gran in Scotland live anywhere near the Northumberland coast?' I asked Jane McLachlan casually. 'We're going up there for Easter to stay in our cottage by the sea. We might be able to see each other in the holidays.'

'Yes, she lives near Berwick,' answered Jane, beaming. 'You can come and visit us, Charlie, and I'll show you round the farm.'

Angela gave me a push. 'Take no notice of her, Jane,' she sneered. 'She hasn't got a cottage by the sea in Northumberland. She's making it up.'

'So what's that then, Miss Cleverbloomers Mitchell?' I said. 'Scotch mist?' And I took out the photos of the cottage and showed them round.

Angela was furious. She was so mad she didn't speak to me for the rest of the day. But that didn't bother me. It served her right, and I didn't care if she never spoke to me again.

I packed up my belongings at home time and walked out of school without her, looking forward to a peaceful holiday by the sea and to spending some time with Jane, who may not be as adventurous as Angela but who's definitely a whole lot nicer.

But before I left I did one last thing. I got Angela's brand new expensive pink Beebop

trainers from her locker. I carried them round
the back of the school to where the caretaker
had just had a heap of coal delivered for the
boiler. I rubbed the trainers in the coal dust
until they were black and filthy all over. Then
I flung them back into her locker and walked
out.

I'm not usually like that, but people can
only take so much of Angela's kind of mischief.
And I'd decided that this time I'd really had
enough.